Legacies Are Forever
Book 3

by

Richard Neil LaBute Jr.

DORRANCE PUBLISHING CO
EST. 1920
PITTSBURGH, PENNSYLVANIA 15238

The contents of this work, including, but not limited to, the accuracy of events, people, and places depicted; opinions expressed; permission to use previously published materials included; and any advice given or actions advocated are solely the responsibility of the author, who assumes all liability for said work and indemnifies the publisher against any claims stemming from publication of the work.

All Rights Reserved
Copyright © 2018 by Richard Neil LaBute Jr.

No part of this book may be reproduced or transmitted, downloaded, distributed, reverse engineered, or stored in or introduced into any information storage and retrieval system, in any form or by any means, including photocopying and recording, whether electronic or mechanical, now known or hereinafter invented without permission in writing from the publisher.

Dorrance Publishing Co
585 Alpha Drive
Suite 103
Pittsburgh, PA 15238
Visit our website at *www.dorrancebookstore.com*

ISBN: 978-1-4809-4789-4
eISBN: 978-1-4809-4812-9

Dedication

This book is dedicated to Daniel R. Quernemon, a devout Christian man who I very much admire and who, many years ago, recognized prospect and characteristics in me by hiring me for my first post- service, civilian job. Under Dan's mentorship, I was sent on my second and third "embassy" to Japan which afforded me the opportunity to improve my understandings of the language, culture and rich history of a people and a nation.

Preface

The Struggle has ended. Hundreds of thousands molder in early graves, fallen by shot, shell and disease. Still more are displaced, homeless, or maimed after four, long years of fratricide. To the victor goes the spoils, yet the Union armies have succeeded only in stamping out a cause lost already many years before the first shot sounded at Fort Sumter. The exhausted antagonists stand down, almost in disbelief that the horrible nightmare of war is finally at an end. Yet some on both sides desire to carry on the fight, those either in denial, or seeking revenge, or simply overcome by a blood lust that cannot be quenched by word, ink and parchment. Most soldiers, whether blue or grey, regular or irregular, go home. Others offer their guns and experience to high bidders such a Maximillian of Mexico or anonymity in the *Legion d'Etrangere* of France. Yet the globe does not spin on the axis of North America, change abounds everywhere in the late, middle years of the 19th century.

In Japan, young, liberal heirs to centuries-old fiefdoms unite to bring about the end to the Tokugawa Shogunate. The two hundred fifty year reign of Tokugawa military rule is over. The

Restoration has brought the Meiji Emperor out of the secluded confines of Kyoto and back to the center of government and power in old Yedo, now Tokyo. The *Sonno Joi*, revere the Emperor, expel the barbarians, movement has succeeded yet failed. The Shogun is gone, but the hated *bakufu*, Tokugawa-era government bureaucrats, remain. The Sun of Heaven, that is the Meiji Emperor, less of a demi-god now than in the time of his future grandson some fifty years hence, promulgates western-style change, or adaptations thereof, but remains in a consultative, Head of State role. Japan as a nation quickly sheds its medieval past, rapidly emulates, then seizes a place at the table of modern nations, much to the dismay and expense of its neighbors, north, south, west and ultimately the United States and its possessions to the east.

In Europe, Prussia, with the help of Bavaria cements together a Germanic nation, as France tends to its colonies on many continents. The three-hundred-year-old Romanov Russian Empire teeters of the brink of disaster and revolution. Equally decrepit empires of the Ottoman Turks, Austro-Hungarians, and Ching dynasty of China also near their end. The riddance of imperial overlords, national identity, and the power of the proletariat are themes *du jour*, of the day.

Chapter One

Memories of Jiro

When, no how did I become old? *Ryojin*, aged one, this is what the younger generations call me today. These young people all bow low with purposeful ceremony, but their disdain of my irrelevance is all too evident.

Although my memories are many; trial and error, victory and failure, I feel no different in my heart today than when I attained manhood.

At age sixteen, in the stable and service of my liege, Lord Sumida of Gonohe, we "boys" were gathered together for recognition and a solemn blessing on the occasion of our "coming of age." The chief and resident *kannoshi*, Shinto priest, of the great shrine made an appearance to sanctify the event. As he entered the great hall of Lord Sumida's manor, his impressive entourage of *omikosan*, priestly attendants, were a testament to the importance and richness of "his" shrine. All this as if he, a mere priest, whose shrine stands at the forgotten end of the great North-South road, could compete with the lineage, prestige and power of my liege Lord!

As he passed me, his eyes fixed upon me, knowingly, slightly acknowledging me and our many hours spent together in study of history and the scriptures. He dare not interfere with the business and governance of Lord Sumida. Still he could not help feeling somewhat cheated when I was called away to Lord Sumida's service along with a nagging sense of being deceived and used by me as I had feigned interest in religious affairs, raising his expectations of a priestly prospect. Deceived? How could he have deceived himself that I would have been satisfied cloistered away into a life of mantras and chants in a shrine in the *michinoku*, end of the road, district of northern Japan.

On the occasion, the ceremony seemed to drone on forever. Yet, today, I possess only the most fleeting memories of it. Still, I ask myself, where are they all now?

The vastly rich, powerful and feared Lord Sumida, he is long since dead and gritty ash upon a funeral pyre. The chief priest, he stands in stony effigy, draped in red, communing, no doubt, with the spirits and saints he so longed to be with in life. Goh, the beastly assistant martial arts instructor, he failed to serve his liege on the field of battle, rather choked to death on a chunk of grisly meat snatched from a serving of *chankonabe*, a mixed stew of meat, vegetables and broth often fed to sumo wrestlers. Goh was no sumoist, just the most aggressive partaker of Lord Sumida's sustenance and bounty. Oh, how I would have loved to witness Goh first turning red, then blue, eyes bulging from their sockets, gasping and finally realizing that this, his death, would turn out to be as unexceptional as his life. There he lies, a great, beached leviathan in the center of the *dojo*, martial arts practice ring, dead.

And finally, all of us "boys," the young students in military and administrative training at Lord Sumida's manor, they, like me, those who still walk this earth, surviving only with our memories and a pitiful pension of *ichibu*, silver coins, for sustenance in the waning days of our lives.

"Ueno-*sama*, polite honorific, Ueno-sama. A letter, a letter addressed to you, but it's not from Japan!"

"Calm down, Takito-*san*, standard honorific, calm down. Let me see what you have there before either of us become overly excited. Yes, you are correct, it is a letter. A letter addressed to me, a letter postmarked Washington, D.C., United States of America. How very strange! Who would know me from Washington, D.C.? Well, let's see what it says."

Ueno Jiro-sama,

You may not remember me. It has been over a decade since we last met. My name is Thomas Bayard. We first met in Philadelphia. I was then assistant to Secretary of State William Marcy. If you may recall, we had quite a time touring the United States together, you and I and your two colleagues. Secretary Marcy died not long after you returned to Japan, but I have remained in the government, though not in the Department of State. During our late war, I served for a period of time with the navy. It was boring work, some in port and some in blockade duty along the eastern coast of the Confederacy. After the war many of my fellow officers were mustered out of the service, but I remained with the Navy Department as a civilian, due in part to my previous position with Secretary Marcy at State.

Presently, I am with the Bureau of Ordnance, a department within the Navy Department. I apologize for boring you with a history of my government service, so I'll move along to the point of this letter.

Your visit to our country was, and remains unique in our fledgling national relations. In my capacity at State and through correspondence with the former Representative Minister to the Japanese court, Mr. Pruyn, I managed to follow some of your government service. How exciting it must have been to be at the center of a revolution and then the rapid modernization of your country. The current Ambassador, the Hon. Robert Van Valkenburgh, assisted me with the delivery of this letter.

In my capacity within the Bureau of Ordnance, I have been charged with the sale and disposal of surplus war materiel including ex-Confederate naval stores. Such "stores" include vessels of the ex-Confederate Navy. Among the wrecks, and derelict hulks, one vessel stands out as of particular interest, the ex-CSS Stonewall, a fearsome ram built for riverine or coastal waters use. The vessel is practically new, never having fired a shot during the late war. It seemed to me that such a warship would be of great value to your government in its efforts to modernize, especially given your coastal and inland waterways.

I am enclosing a basic drawing of the vessel, along with a list of specifications and armaments. I am authorized to offer the complete warship to your government for $500,000 in gold. It is my hope that should *your government express interest in the purchase, that I may have the opportunity to travel to your country and to meet you again.*

I look forward to your reply by return.

Your humble servant,
Thomas Bayard, Bureau of Ordnance

"Thank you, Takito-san. I should like to be alone now. *Sayonara*, goodbye." Hmh, how very interesting! There is still rebellion in Kyushu as well as Hokkaido. A western, "ironclad" warship could be most useful, now against these diehards, later, perhaps in convincing "neighbors" of our mostly "peaceful" intentions. The Western Powers' foreign policies have always been heavily weighted toward colonialism and the projection of power. Japan is surrounded on three sides, not with indigenous governments, but with colonial and proxy organizations without long-term objectives and little regard for local people. For the present, Japan must run with this pack of dogs or continue to languish in isolation. In the "near" future however, these white devils can be displaced, due in no small part, by their own contempt for the colored peoples of the world, a world which they now control. A strong Japan can lead if not dominate an economic sphere from Sakhalin to the East Indies, and as far west as India. Perhaps this is Japan's destiny? I have been far too myopic. There is much work to be done!

Chapter Two
The Beast

Japan! Well, I'll be a yellow monkey's ass. This will be the third time in my fifty years that I'll be bound for those craggy shores beneath snow-capped volcanic peaks crawling with those kowtowing, smiling, murderous Jappers. As a young'un, little Davie, from Leonardstown, I never thought travelling to the Japans. I could never have imagined watching them bandy-legged samurai shits strutting along like God created the world for their pleasure, then helping them fight their wars. God, I wonder if Pruyn is still in Yedo. I believe that I read somewhere that our diplomatic presence there has been upgraded to an official embassy, now that the Emperor has returned to Yedo. Pruyn, an ambassador! I can still see him, trousers around his ankles, knelling on the floor of that teahouse banging that young Japper girl. I think I'd enjoy it more this time than I did then. I was always too worried about proprieties. I'm too old for proprieties anymore. How long has it been since I had any woman anyway? Maybe a short run to Japan might be good for me. I'll read the order once again, more slowly to make certain my old eyes are not deceiving me.

TO: Captain David S. McDougal
FM: Secretary of the Navy

Upon receipt of this order, you shall proceed to Havana Harbor, Cuba to, on behalf of the United States Government, take possession of the ex-Confederate warship CSS Stonewall. A skeleton crew shall be provided by the first available U.S. warship. Upon arrival of said temporary crew, proceed directly to Mobile Harbor, State of Alabama. There you will take on, ex-Confederate Capt. Page, formerly the CSS Stonewall's Commanding Officer, as Technical Advisor and await the arrival of representatives of the Japanese government. A full, regular navy crew will also assemble and report aboard at Mobile. Once Capt. Page, the Japanese representative(s) and your crew have reported aboard, you are to proceed directly to Tokyo Harbor, Japan via Cape Horn and the Sandwich Islands. Within a reasonable time you are to make any necessary repairs, train the crew and supply the vessel for the journey. A full accounting of expenses related to said repair, training and supply must be provided to the Hon. Robert Van Valkenburgh, United States Ambassador to Japan. Ambassador Van Valkenburgh will, in turn, authorize release of the vessel to the Government of Japan at the appropriate time. Godspeed,

Gideon Welles, Secretary of the Navy

Well, it's just a matter of packing my sea-bag then. Umm, let's see; a couple of days to finalize details here and at the Navy Department, a week in transit to Havana, I'd better plan to go by sea, the Southern railways are still a mess from the war. I do believe Sherman enjoyed that march of his to the sea. He sure seems to hate railroads! I wonder how many years it will take before rail travel is reliable south of the Mason-Dixon Line? Anyway, a few days in Havana to be sure, with Spanish bureaucrats nothing is ever straightforward. A week to steam back to Mobile, where I'll no doubt remain for some weeks waiting for the Captain Page, the Japanese representatives and my crew. While in Washington outbound, I'll pay a visit to the Office of Detail (designation for the U.S. Navy Personnel Department until 1942) and see who of my old colleagues may be in the Mobile or Pensacola area. I'll need some distraction if it's an extended stay. And no Pruyn! The telegram mentions Ambassador Van Valkenburgh. I can make some subtle queries around Washington, but I don't suppose to expect someone like Pruyn again. Transit time to Japan, around the Horn with resupply in Rio de Janeiro, Brazil, Montevideo, Uruguay and Concepcion on Chile's west coast.

Some several days later Captain McDougal arrives at the Navy Yard located in the southeastern reaches of the Washington along the Anacostia River. The main gate, located at 8th and M Streets is an historic edifice even in 1868. Wrought iron, colonnades, hipped roof, flanked by two white-painted brick guard lodges, imposing and impressive.

"Atten-hut!"

"Good afternoon, Captain. How may I be of service to you, sir?" asks the young Marine Corporal of the Guard.

"Thank you, Corporal. I am here to call on a civilian, a Mr. Thomas Bayard. I believe he can be found in the Administrative Building?"

"One moment, sir." The corporal withdraws to the guard lodge wherein he checks the book of personnel and locations. After a moment he confidently returns to the captain.

"Yes, sir. Mr. Bayard, a civilian with the Bureau of Ordnance. He is located in the Administrative Building, south across the park. It is a larger building with six sash windows and brick quoins. You can't miss it, sir."

"Thank you, Corporal. I'm sure I'll find my way."

The Corporal stiffly salutes, casually returned by Captain McDougal.

A few minutes later Captain McDougal arrives at the handsome Administrative Building. He enters and is greeted by a uniformed receptionist.

"Good afternoon, sir. How may I assist you?"

"Looking for Mr. Bayard. If he is available, would you tell him Captain McDougal requests a few moments of his time?"

"Yes, sir. One moment, sir." The Seaman scurries down the hallway. A few moments later he returns in the wake of Mr. Bayard rushing out to greet Captain McDougal.

"Ah, the famous Captain McDougal, hero of the Battle of Shimonoseki. A pleasure to meet you, sir."

McDougal is momentarily taken back. Regaining his composure, he replies, "The hero of Shimonoseki? I don't recall being called that before. I failed in my mission to locate and close with the CSS Alabama. The Alabama passed me during the night in the Sunda Straits in the Dutch East Indies. The battle of Shimonoseki was merely a distraction which cost me a number of my men and several weeks lost to repairs!"

"A brutal appraisal of yourself, Captain McDougal. On the contrary, your collaborations in Japan helped bring about changes in that country, which our bilateral relations will benefit from for years to come. And your mission against the Alabama was part of a multi-pronged seek and destroy mission. It just so happened that she was ultimately cornered in Cherbourg, France by the USS Kearsarge, and in this case Captain Pickering gets the laurel, but it does not in any way diminish the role you and the Wyoming played in her demise!"

"Mr. Bayard, I'm beginning to like you. I like the way you think! I don't necessarily agree with you, you understand. But I do like this way you think. Now Mr. Bayard, by strange circumstance I am here on another matter which relates to the Japans."

"Yes, Captain, I know. Unbeknownst to you I was a player in the first chapter of this saga, and now the initiator of the second."

"What in the name of hell are you talking about?" asks McDougal clearly puzzled.

"Before the war I was with State. As an assistant to then Secretary Marcy, I was charged with handling three state guests from Japan, brought here by Commodore Perry. We spent several weeks together. One of those guests has, through the years, become well placed in the Japanese government. During the war and your mission to Japan and Asia, the man of whom I speak may have played a role in communications and relations with the court of the Shogun. Now, today, he may be playing a role in the purchase of the ex-Confederate warship Stonewall, which is the purpose of your visit today, is it not, sir?"

"By God, Bayard, you have found me out. You know of my orders then? What insight can you then offer, which could help me on this mission?"

"Particular insights, none. But I get orders too. I am to accompany you! I am to be the official liaison with both the American diplomatic personnel abroad and our Japanese guests aboard. We are to make ready, ferry, and deliver 'The Beast' to Japan."

"Well, my prerogatives seem to diminish by the minute. A liaison, a technical advisor and an undetermined number of Jappers in addition to officers and crew with whom I am not familiar, as we steam a shallow-draft riverine vessel around the Horn and across the blue waters of the Pacific. The "hero" of Shimonoseki, that's not what I'll be called after this mission, if we make it. At best, I'll be hailed as Circus Master McDougal and his naval menagerie! All right Mr. Thomas Bayard, Bureau of Ordnance, let us weigh anchor and move the flag to Havana. I'm anxious to see 'The Beast' of which we speak."

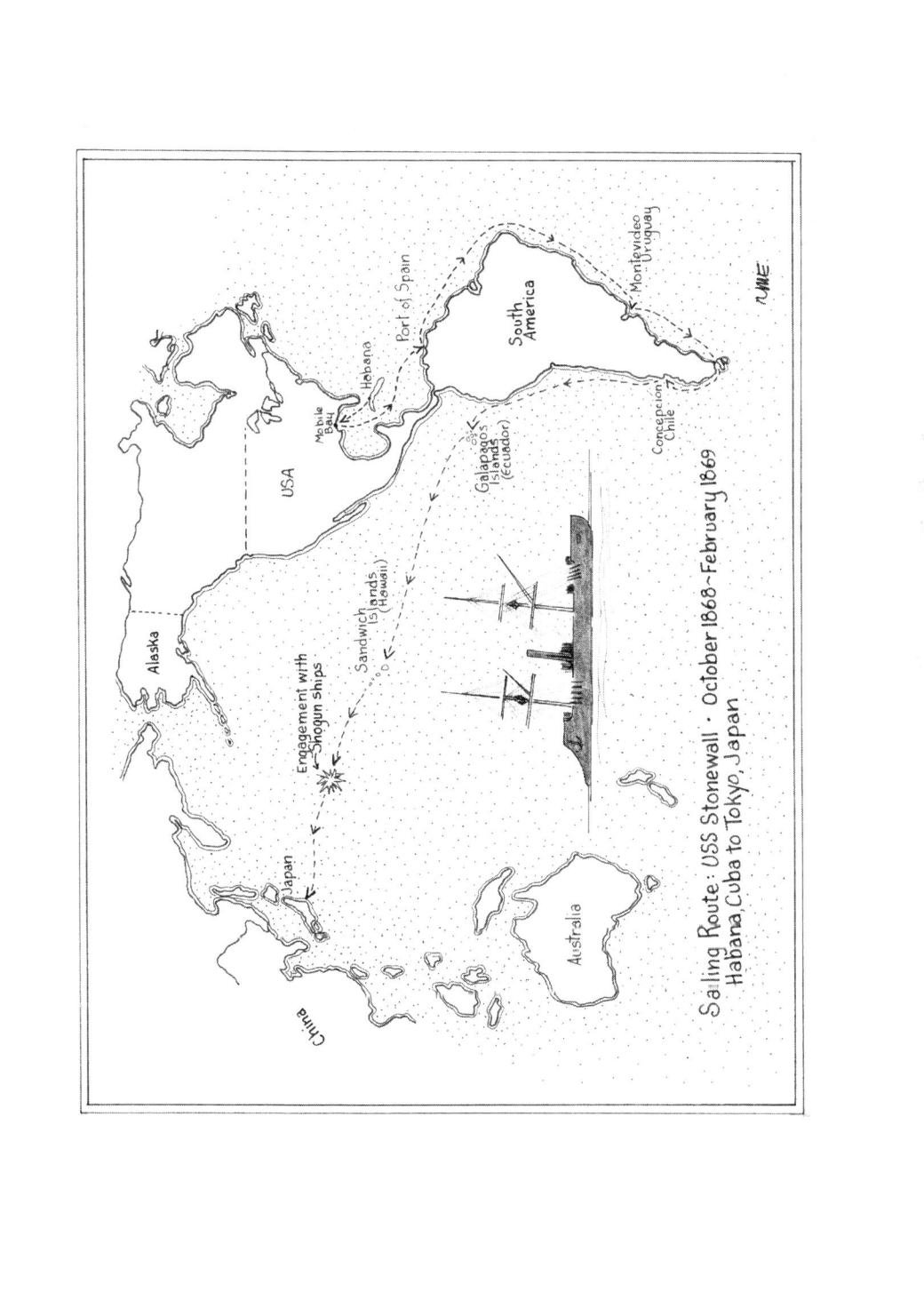

Sailing Route: USS Stonewall · October 1868–February 1869
Habana, Cuba to Tokyo, Japan

Chapter Three
The Waiting

The 13th *Daimyo* Mori Takachika, Prince of Nagato, Lord of the Choshu is dead by his own hand. He has entered the house of his ancestors. In death, he has honored the clan. He lived to the death, *bushido*, the way of the warrior. Yet, the spirits of the clan are not at peace, they are restless. Takachika produced no heir in his time among the living. He is the last *daimyo* in the lineage. Lady Mori, or Lady Chizuru as she prefers to be addressed, barren by childhood sickness, rules the clan by proxy through aged Counsellor Takahashi. By age, disease and incessant skirmishing, male heirs to the Lordship of the Mori clan are all dead. The clan as a political entity will be dissolved; its lands, people and assets forfeit to the Imperial Throne, later to be distributed in gifting to faithful and supportive fiefdoms. Lady Chizuru only waits, as the others, to learn the fates of the fiefdom, her person, and the answer to the secret message sent so many weeks before to the imperial court.

Lord Mori's uncle, and cavalry commander, Akane, is also dead. He was cut down in the first melee of the Battle of Shimonoseki. Already half-forgotten, he fell in the field near a shrine along the great East-West road. His skirmish with the French, a mere side-show in the amphibious assault in the Battle of Shimonoseki. Still the junior officers of his cavalry unit remember. They remember the power of the French weapons, the sudden death of their commander, soon followed his lieutenant, comrades dying and wounded, the withdrawal - no retreat and the humiliating surrender of Lord Mori's forces to the *gaijin*, foreigners.

"I've had enough!" loudly complains one young officer to a group gathered together. "Our liege is dead. Our commander is dead. We are ordered to stand-down under imperial decree. We are no longer *samurai*, warriors. We are *ryonin*, unemployed, masterless *samurai*. Worse than worthless. We are the living dead."

"If I had enough courage I would kill myself." chimes in one of the group. "Let us ride north into the wilder country. We can take from the dim-witted peasants what we need, what we want. We will eat their rice, drink their *sake*, rice wine, fuck their women. To the north, the territories of the *daimyo* are expansive and undeveloped. The great wars and great armies of the *daimyo* are long since passed. What troops the fiefdoms retain have moved south in support of the Emperor. Towns, villages and roads are, no doubt, manned only by local conscripts. We can slice through these like fresh *tofu*, white bean curd."

"We will be hunted and killed," cautions one of the group.

"We will fight. We will be men again. Eventually all men die. But we will die as *samurai*. We will die as we choose, by the sword, not as dogs laying here waiting to be fed."

"I agree. Let us take our chances as men, not as women and dogs. To the north!" forcefully yells another.

Lady Chizuru can sense the tension, present in all those in and outside of the court. Boredom born of the waiting, stretches like a bad note plucked from a string, hanging in the air, one that will not dissipate with the wind. When his lordship lived, she would stand silently in the background watching and listening, gathering images and words to be carefully processed and understood at a later time. Now she watches and listens, but sees little and hears less. The court of Hagi castle, the people of the Choshu domain go about their mundane existence fearing. Under his lordship they feared the given, his temper and whimsical acts of violence. Now they fear the unknown, the unimagined.

In her prayers and in her heart Lady Chizuru can still find peace. The peace of the God of the Cross comforts her. She remembers the words "I am with thee." Even in the uncertainty and fear that is "the waiting," she experiences a strong urging that is a desire to share with others, all others. After the great *jishin*, earthquake, she organized aid and sustenance to his lordship's people. He grumbled and berated her gesture to his people but made no attempt to interfere. She ponders this "urging." Certainly all people require shelter and sustenance but do not their fragile souls require soothing also? Can people really live a life with a scarred and troubled soul? Is not this the basis for wandering ghosts and angry spirits who inhabit the world just beyond our understanding?

This very pre-dawn morning, as Lady Chizuru tries to reconcile her thoughts, she hears voices and quieted horses shuffling in the courtyard.

"Be quieter. I am certain we may have been heard. We must be long gone before anyone can pays us mind," urges the organizing lieutenant, Lieutenant Goemon, of the cavalry band.

Through the gates, onto the main road leading to the southeast, then quickly off on a lesser travelled road to the north canter a band of eleven junior officers, senior ranks and their pack animals to an anticipated life of storied brigandry somewhere in the wilds of northern Japan.

"Free air in my lungs, the brightening sky and the fading stars above, I am revived already," says one of the group out loud without really speaking to anyone.

They travel quickly, hardly without banter, and after four hours they rest in a well-watered grove.

"How far have we come?" asks one of the group without really addressing anyone.

"I measure it at near eight *ri*, Japanese unit of measure, 1 *ri* equaling about 4 km. We are approaching the village of Abumachi. When we pass, don't look hurried or haphazard. We will maintain our mounts in rank file at a walk, very professional, very military. I wish to draw no attention to us. By trying to circumvent the village or hurrying through, every tongue would whisper, why?" explains Lieutenant Goemon.

The passage through the village proves uneventful. A handful of villagers, peddlers and country peasants pay scant attention to the cavalry formation. About ½ *ri* north of Abumachi, Goemon's worse nightmare appears blocking the road to the front of his column in small unit infantry formation. Banners flapping in the breeze indicate imperial guards. It is an understrength infantry unit, but the shining razor-like edges of the *yari*, traditional Japanese pike, and spears form a formidable barrier to a cavalry unit. Goemon spins his horse to the left intending to call for a quick withdrawal back toward Abumachi, then onto a peasant track to the northeast or east. Fate does not permit an easy escape. To the rear he finds another small unit forming up just outside of town. They too are armed with *yari* and spears. He loudly addresses the group.

"Must be the same unit! To the west are rice paddies, then the sea. To the east are more rice paddies, difficult terrain for horses and pack animals. They know this! We cannot go back. We cannot wheel left or right. We must charge the formation, break through and run." Lieutenant Goemon pulls his *katana* from its sheath, as do the others. They charge the formation blocking the road to their front.

"Ai-ya!" screams Lieutenant Goemon.

"Ai-ya!" scream the others.

The blocking unit is temporarily stunned by Goemon's act of madness. Nothing happens without orders and orders are slow to come as the commanding lieutenant stands starring with his mouth open. Seconds elapse.

"Prepare to repel cavalry!" finally escapes the defending lieutenant's mouth.

Too late! Goemon and two others have already penetrated the thin infantry line and burst out its back, slicing and hacking the infantrymen on their way through. The well-trained unit does not disintegrate, however. It quickly reforms to the center and presents the rest of Goemon's group with a wall of pike and spear tips. Unable to maneuver due to the narrow road and encumbered by the pack animals, the remaining eight cavalrymen attempt to fight off the infantry while mounted. It is a quick and uneven fight. The cavalrymen and their valuable mounts are systematically butchered. In less than five minutes the fight is over and Goemon's group lies dead and dismembered on the road and its shoulder. All the supplies are forfeit. For the moment all of this is lost on the young lieutenant as he flees at breakneck pace up the road, headed north.

"If only this waiting were to end!" laments Lady Chizuru to her most intimate handmaiden Etsuko.

As if by the force of magic, a call from the gate sentry is heard, an official rider is approaching.

Chapter Four
Arrangements

"Ah, Captain Sugiyama, what a pleasant surprise. And a Mr., I am sorry I am not familiar with your name, sir," greets Ambassador Van Valkenburgh.

"Thank you, Ambassador, my name is Ueno, Jiro Ueno. I am Captain Sugiyama's official interpreter. I am here in a supportive role, just to make certain nothing is lost in translation with the American ambassador.

"I see, this is not a social call then, is it Captain Sugiyama?" questions Ambassador Van Valkenburgh.

"*Gomen nasai*, I am sorry, Ambassador Van Valkenburgh, **I** English is **no** good **with** Ueno-san."

"Yes, Captain Sugiyama, I understand. Your English is **not as good as** Ueno-san's English. No matter, between the three of us, I am certain that we can conduct business on behalf of our respective governments.

"Yes, certainly so," agrees Captain Sugiyama.

"Years ago, sir, Captain Sugiyama and I had the pleasure of working with then Ambassador Pruyn and one of your naval commanders during the Shimonoseki incident and the Choshu insurrection," begins Ueno.

"Ah, yes. Pruyn and the Battle of Shimonoseki. I have been briefed about the incidents," recalls Van Valkenburgh. "As I was briefed, all of us did quite well by taking the wind out of the sails of that uppity warlord as well as pocketing his substantial treasury.

"Uppity?" queries Ueno.

"Yes, 'uppity' is defined as someone acting above his station. Some petty person, out of his class," expounds the ambassador.

"Ambassador, Lord Mori was not a petty warlord. Lord Mori was a great lord, the hieratical leader of the Mori *han*, clan. Unfortunately he was also a brigand and an organizer and powerful supporter of the *Sonno Joi* movement which ultimately led to revolution in our country. Although he is dead, the spirit of his movement remains influential with rebellious forces in both the northern and southern extremes of the country. His lasting impact is one of the reasons we are gathered here today," mildly scolds Ueno-san.

"Yes, yes, I see. Sorry to have inferred insult on this popular brigand. In my country, we just hang outlaws and be done with it!" sarcastically interjects the Ambassador.

"In your country, ancient and noble families do not exist!" adds Ueno beginning to show some emotion.

Sensing tensions rising on both sides, the normally xenophobic Captain Sugiyama interjects, "Yes, Ambassador, Hokkaido and Kyushu *daimyo* cause much trouble. We, Japanese Navy, wish to purchase from Americans the warship Stonewall. Stonewall cause *daimyo* much trouble!"

"The Stonewall. What is the name of God is the Stonewall?" asks Van Valkenburgh more than surprised.

Ueno quickly proffers the Thomas Bayard letter. Van Valkenburgh briefly scans the unexpected document.

"I have not been so informed through official channels, Captain Sugiyama. I will, rather I can, do nothing until I receive specific instruction from my government."

"We have our bureaucracies too, Mr. Ambassador. But what we are requesting is that you communicate my receipt of the letter, and extend our unofficial interest in the subject. Once an official offer is extended, obviously through your good offices, Mr. Ambassador, Japan will act swiftly to accept the offer. With your invitation, Captain Sugiyama and I will then make travel arrangements to the United States for the purpose of escorting the vessel back here to Tokyo where an exchange can be made," summarizes "Interpreter" Ueno.

"I will make an immediate query as to the validity of the matter. May I be of any further service to you gentlemen today?" asks Van Valkenburgh icily and without any interest in further discussions.

"No, Mr. Ambassador. This concludes our business today. Thank you for your time and assistance with the matter," politely extends Interpreter Ueno.

Van Valkenburgh, detesting to have been caught unaware, and cursing his own lack of information, offers a tentative and limp parting handshake. Both Japanese men bow only. All take their leave without the warm glow of diplomatic niceties. Returning to his office within the embassy, Van Valkenburgh clears his desk in order to pen a letter to Secretary of State William Henry Steward. In doing so, he notices an official letter from the Secretary near the top of his incoming mail. Lifting his eyes toward the heavens and letting out a groan, he slices the envelope open, extracts the contents and reads it carefully.

FM: Secretary of State WH Steward
TO: Ambassador Robert Van Valkenburgh
SUBJ: Trans-Pacific Trade

Ambassador Van Valkenburgh, it is the expressed desire of the Grant Administration to promote regional stability and increase trans-pacific trade, specifically with the new government of Japan as well as with China and other lesser powers in the region. Increased American trade, thereby American presence will, without doubt, contribute to greater American influence throughout the region. The Administration understands the current problem with a general lack of hard currency and the local preferences for Spanish or Mexican silver. The Administration intends to propose to Congress a Coinage Act, whereby excess American silver will be minted for the expressed use in the Oriental markets. This type of legislation, of course, may take some time, and as you know the Administration has its priorities and Congress has theirs. What the Spanish and Mexicans lack however are manufactured goods and services to sell. In the interests of bi-lateral relations as well as the stability of the new Japanese government, the Navy Department and the War Department have been authorized to sell surplus, non-strategic and ex-Confederate materials of war to Japan in order to aid the new governments in its efforts to strengthen the national Army & Navy, and unify the country. Letters have been dispatched from the Navy's Ordnance Department and the Army's Quartermasters Department to this end. Your office shall provide all assistance to these efforts, further acting as principal in the absence of official delegations, draw-up contracts, conduct transactions and accept payment on behalf of the United States. Should questions arise, as they are certain to, use your good judgement and experience to conduct and close these matters on behalf of your government. You may request clarification and additional instructions at any time without prejudice.

Good luck Robert.
William H Steward, Secretary

"Oh, for the love of God! Had I only read my mail before entertaining official guests," muses Van Valkenburgh. "What to do? Alright, Robert, first, you'll pen letters to both Navy Ordnance and Army Quartermaster, offering all assistance with their surplus and disposal directives. Second, I'll invite Captain Sugiyama and his interpreter to a proper dinner, querying them as to their military hardware and training needs, but only after a suitable number of bi- lateral toasts, offering the best Scotch whiskey to be procured within the diplomatic community here in Tokyo. Confidences regained and equilibriums restored, I'll execute my own instructions without anyone ever knowing how I nearly fucked it up. No complaints, no congressional enquiries, no recall. Robert Van Valkenburgh, Ambassador, remains in office another day!"

Chapter Five
Founding Fathers

"The Shogun is gone. The Son of Heaven is with us. All which we have worked and hoped for has been attained. On us, we Four, lies the awesome responsibility to reform this nation," cites Okubo Toshimichi, the new Home Minister and foremost leader of the Oligarchy.

"All is not yet settled Okubo-san. There are many who oppose fundamental change, many from your own *han*, clan of Satsuma. Government offices are filled with old *bakufu*, bureaucrats, from Tokyo to the smallest hamlet in the land. They resist giving up their place at the trough," cautions Ito Hirobumi a recently returned graduate of University College London.

"A new era dawns in Japan. *Sakoku*, the Tokugawa-era isolation policy, has left Japan two hundred years behind western nations in terms of science and industrialization. Old ways will have to change, old men will have to change. It will be difficult for many to put treasured customs aside. However, customs and disagreement among men does not mean civil war," postulates Okubo.

"Japan is a nation of warriors and has a history of civil war. Three hundred *daimyo*, great and small, and all their retainers vie for prestige and influence," adds Kido Takayoshi, Imperial Advisor. "Ambitions and egos will not easily be put aside."

"When we left Japan, we all were under penalty of death. There are those who think us corrupted by western influences and traitors to *bushido* and the motherland. It takes time to change a heart," notes Ito.

"Yes, I know, Ito-san. Confucius says, '*Only the wisest and stupidest men change.*' Those thousands of swords and spears in the middle scare you. But what is it that we have struggled and fought for? Our Japan or theirs?" Remember, Ito-san, '*he who exercises government by means of virtue may be compared to the north polar star, which keeps it place and all other stars turn toward it,*'" philosophizes Okubo quoting Confucius.

"Well, spoken, Okubo-san. But sophistry does not change the facts. Facts which we must deal with on a daily basis. First, we must consolidate imperial control of all Japanese lands. Honshu, the center of Japan, is bracketed by rebellious fiefdoms in both Kyushu to the south and Hokkaido to the north. Our own 'armies' and those of like-minded *daimyo* are no substitute for imperial troops. Presently the Emperor maintains only a small house guard which is supplemented by our own men! We must build an imperial army and build it soon. Incidents such as the attempted escape of some of the late Lord Mori's men are on the rise. We surmise that they were trying to join forces with other malcontent, and rebellious forces in the north."

"Mori's men! He was of our generation, but identified with old ways," interjects Kido.

"No, Kido, Mori Takachika identified only with himself. He was *bushi*, samurai, on the outside, *akaoni*, red devil demi-god (particularly self-serving), on the inside," quips Okubo. "Now to today's business. We have noted the need to build an imperial army as soon as possible. To this end, our own troops can serve as the nucleus of such a land-based force. We need to look however at a navy, which none of our four fiefdoms possess. Western doctrine calls for a combined and coordinated effort between the army and the navy in many battle scenarios, particularly those involving a nation of islands such as ours. Sanpans filled with sword-wielding retainers and archers are not the basis of a navy, as we saw in Shimonoseki. We will require armored, steam-driven vessels with modern naval guns. The western nations are eager to trade with us, let them trade weapons of war," says Okubo.

Practical Ito talks reality to the group. "Money will be an issue. True, the western nations are eager to trade with Japan, but resource poor as we are, we have little to trade with. In the days of the 'black ships,' the Portuguese were almost as interested in proselytizing their Christian faith as they were in trading goods for Japanese silver, which ultimately brought about the Shimabara Rebellion, the banning of Christianity, and two hundred fifty years of *sakoku* policy of the Shogunate."

Silent throughout the discussion so far, Saigo Takamori, deep in his own thought chimes in.

"These Americans are Christians also. Our experiences, though limited, indicate that they and their missionaries are even more zealous than were the Portuguese. For the lack of our silver, perhaps this is the gate to the ends we seek? Religious fervor emasculates men. They blindly seek something not of this earth. They bleat and pray without really expecting intersession. They are obedient. They can be easily controlled. After the Shimabara Rebellion when the Portuguese missionaries were expelled and their followers were made to renounce their faith or be executed like their god of the cross, tens of thousands accepted death upon the cross, praying and crying. Men, crying!"

"Agreed! We use this Christianity as bait. But we still require gold," reminds Okubo. "Taxes and revenue are a major problem. The *gaijin* will not trade for rice and peasants. Japan is plentiful only in these. Some taxes are collected on former Tokugawa lands, but with the Shogun gone, his tax collectors often collect for the highest bidder, and the highest bidders are quick to forget any obligation to a central authority, even in the name of the Son of Heaven."

"You are correct, Okubo-san, we need not empty our storehouses of rice or gather in peasants like corn in the summer. Ozawa may be our answer!" adds Saigo.

"Ozawa?" questions all.

"Yes, Ozawa. North on the Tohoku road, then west of Fukushima, hidden in the mountains, there is a mine. From this mine the old regime had been extracting gold. Not loudly or with fanfare, not in a *tsunami* of diggers, but constantly and consistently for many years," continues Saigo.

"How is it that you know of this mine and we do not, Saigo?" asks Kido.

"The old regime subsisted on informants and spies. Many in the land are hungry. Fill their rice bowls and you may be surprised as to what they share."

"With incentives and gold, we shall buy western weapons of war," concludes Okubo. All agree. "Next, call for Ueno Jiro. I understand he has landed us a big fish!"

"One more item, Okubo-san," raises Kido. "Prior to the *seppuku*, ritual suicide, of Mori Takachika, Lady Mori Chizuru forwarded a message to the imperial court."

"A mere woman, a fish-mongers daughter, petitioning the imperial court!" cries Okubo.

"Outrage!" screams Ito.

"I will slit her from cunt to throat myself," seeths Saigo.

"Unworthy, yes. Outrage, most certainly. But an opportunity to set our trap. She seeks to establish a nunnery. It seems she is a Christian," continues Kido.

"Mori Takachika's widow a Christian? What kind of irony is that!"

Kido continues. "If she were to receive permission from the imperial court to establish her nunnery, it would set into motion all that which we have discussed here today. We rid ourselves of the last vestiges of the Mori *han*, his domain forfeit to the Emperor. By example, the *gaijin* will welcome the gesture and be somewhat less guarded in their negotiations and technology transfers. In the end, should it become bothersome, Christianity can again be outlawed by decree and its flock easily scattered."

"Brilliant, Kido. Prepare the necessary reply in the name of the imperial court," instructs Okubo.

Chapter Six
The Resurrection

Oh, how rapidly the world changes, men are born and die, yet nothing seems to change, still everything changes. Only two decades ago, the mere thought of a journey from Japan to the America, was a notion, if uttered, which could lose a man his head. Yet, it was I who was chosen to conduct that first venture on the American warship Susquehana to and then across a hemisphere, and it is I who shall return to conduct important business on behalf of a new Japan. Is this aging man up to task? Yes, more so now than ever. I am reenergized, I am resurrected from that mass of humanity which busies itself only in the mundane activities of human existence until inevitable sickness and death. I am released to float across the seas with the trade winds, to glide across the untamed and vast open spaces of America, to marvel at its planned cities and revel in its corrupt places. I am alive and free to be Jiro again!

Mr. Thomas Bayard,
  I am in receipt of your letter and unofficial proposal. First, let me express my personal gratitude that

you should remember such a man as myself so many long years and events ago. Second, unofficially on behalf of my government, let me say that, yes, we are interested in acquiring the subject warship pending our full understanding of any further terms and conditions. Upon my government's receipt of your official letter of proposal, you can expect a speedy, positive response. I expect that Captain Sugiyama and I will be sent to your country as an escort to the vessel. I look forward to many pleasant days on our voyage under your tutelage in all things American: customs, written and spoken.

Thank you again. I look forward to working with you again.

Respectfully,

There, the die is cast. I have only to wait for postal time in transit, and the grinding of bureaucratic wheels both here and abroad. This gives me just enough time for necessary consultations and machinations of state here, then to prepare myself for some months abroad. First, Tokyo.

Jiro hurries to the *Kaigunkyoku,* Navy Department Building, within the nascent governmental district of central Tokyo. Captain Sugiyama's small office is not much improved over the old harbor master's hut which he used to share near the wharfs of Yokosuka. Now, however, he finds himself, at least, co-located at the center of naval administration rather than some many *ri* to the south in rural backwaters.

"Captain Sugiyama, it will take us some two weeks direct steaming from Yokohama to San Francisco. There is a new steamship service, The Pacific Mail Steamship Company, operating between Canton, China and San Francisco, primarily engaged in the transportation of excess labor from China to the United States. But these ships do offer better accommodations for business travelers as well as limited, higher-end cargo space. The ships stop in Yokohama for coaling, fresh food and water. You, no doubt, can persuade higher authority to book two, one-way, first-class tickets for us to San Francisco?" suggests Jiro.

"Nothing is decided yet, Ueno-san. Our government has yet to receive an offer, nor accept it in return. These things take time. We must be patient," counsels Sugiyama.

"No, we must gather all available information, anticipate and keep ourselves ahead of events, not be moved along with the events. We know that the offer is to be made through the American Ambassador Van Valkenburgh. We know that our government will accept the offer as speedily as it can without losing face. We must position ourselves at the confluence of these events before they happen. In this manner, we can influence matters on our own terms," insists Jiro.

It is a time of great difficulties in Japan. Before the Tokukawa was the *sengoku*, 150 years of civil strife, incessant fighting between the five leading *daimyo* and their clans. Despised as they were, the Tokugawa brought three centuries of relative peace and seclusion. The Tokugawa represented a known entity. Actions and reactions could be predicted. The new ruling Oligarchy has yet to establish a structured government. Elements of the old regime still rule, governmental bureaucrats continue to go through the motions of administration, the "Four" seek to introduce new ideas and westernization, yet taxation is in chaos. Without money, influence is a hard sell. Edicts and law move with imperial rifles. Imperial rifles are scarce outside the confines of the Tokyo and the imperial palace. Jiro must goad Sugiyama into action, and at the same time manipulate the remaining constants within the new regime to his own ends. Jiro considers his next move.

During the peace of the Tokugawa Shogunate and the *bakufu* bureaucrats, those in comfortable positions of power and even lesser men, resigned themselves to a life without war. Crafty *daimyo*, hardened *bushi*, samurai warriors, and wealthy common men, in the absence of civil strife and as an island nation without borders to defend gradually gave themselves over to more hedonistic pursuits. Such pursuits, known in the *Edo jidai*, Tokugawa Edo era, parlance as the *ukiyo*, the floating world, a world of food, drink and entertainments for all tastes. Jiro, by his nature as well as the demands of his work, was comfortable operating within the shadows of the *ukiyo*. He, himself, would taste its pleasures on occasion, but more often he would use the beguiling influences of a full belly, relaxed tongue, pleasing sights, sounds and a satiated member to effortlessly extract those bits of information so essential in completing the task at hand. But this is a new regime, new men, less corrupt for now, intending new ways. Certainly the *ukiyo* "method" beckones, but Jiro will attempt a less oblique tactic, an American way, a direct appeal to his handlers.

"Gentlemen, may I present Ueno Jiro, a graduate of the *Yushima Seido*, a man of varied talents yet one whose work within the old regime is somewhat less than well documented. A man we can trust?" states Okubo introducing Jiro to the other of the "Four."

Ito is the first to comment. "Ah, Ueno Jiro. I understand, you, like us, have experiences outside the confines of our nation. You have travelled and you speak more than one of the *gaijin* languages? How is it that you have lived so long in this nation of clans and suspicions?"

"As a student of the *Yushima Seido*, under the patronage of my liege Lord Sumida, I was summoned by the *roju*, Tokugawa era ruling council member, to make a voyage to America with the *gaijin* Commodore Perry. Myself and two others were billeted aboard their warships, under strict orders to observe and take notes of everything; language, customs, machinery, and armaments. Honestly, we were not prepared for that which we experienced. We travelled first by warship, then by steam train, by steam riverboat, by civilian passenger ship then warship again. The 'American' race is a mixed stew of many ingredients. They can be collectively brilliant, yet fractured and unharmonious. Their cities shine, and their industrial capacity is awesome. Two of us returned, one died under terrible circumstances. I have lost touch with my friend and companion Nakamori Takeshi, but we served as directed and made a full report of our voyage upon return to our homeland. We were directed to be Japan's first unofficial representatives to the United States, but upon returned we were harshly interrogated, and treated with suspicion. Nevertheless, I have remained in the service of my country."

"Ah, I understand, Ueno-san. These have been difficult times for all of us who love our country and wish to see it respected and represented at the table of nations. Much has transpired since those days of Commodore Perry and his fleet at anchor in Tokyo

Bay. More has changed in Japan in the ensuing dozen or so years than had in the previous three hundred. It has been difficult for some, more difficult for others," adds Okubo almost lamentingly.

Kido continues. "And you are called to sacrifice for your country once again Ueno-san. You are thereby directed to accompany Captain Sugiyama of the Navy Department to the United States and return on the subject warship. Captain Sugiyama will inspect the vessel in port in order to confirm its seaworthiness and to determine its usefulness to the Japanese Navy. Officially, you will work for Captain Sugiyama as his assistant and interpreter. Unofficially, you will report directly to us. This arrangement is not foreign to you, is it, Ueno-san?"

"No, sir, it is not. Actually this arrangement is my preferred manner of engagement."

All "Four" nodding rather than bowing add, "May the gods be with you, 'Interpreter' Ueno."

Jiro slides to his knees, bows deeply with his hands flat and his forehead touching the floor.

Chapter Seven
Habana

In eighteen hundred and sixty-eight, the old Spanish forts and harbor of Habana are imposing and beautiful, even more so to a navy man who appreciates a good, protected deep water anchorage and vintage naval fortifications. As Captain McDougal and his civilian entourage of one, Thomas Bayard, glide through the narrow channel separating the Atlantic from Habana harbor, they pass from one world into another. The air is oppressively hot, and the bright orb overhead burns after only a few minutes of direct contact as they lose the sea spray and refreshing breeze off the Atlantic. Here much is seemingly unchanged in the three centuries of Spanish rule, although the *castile*, fortifications, are beginning to show their age and ensuing years of neglect. Even the Spanish don't expect a piratical invasion from the sea anymore. Jealous or hostile neighbors are a certainly pieces of the "great game," but a direct amphibious assault under the walls and guns of three fortresses is out of the question. Clinging to one of their last New World colonies, the Spanish overlords are suspicious and brutal, and understandably so. *Señor* Carlos Manuel Cespedes and other wealthy Cuban-born planters and gentry have risen up in what will become known as *La Guerra de los diez anos*, the Ten Years War. The colonial masters may blame *los yanquis*, Yankee support and interference, but this is an organic uprising of their own making. It will be ruthlessly suppressed without quarter given.

The Stonewall lay at anchor in *Atares*, one of the three natural bays within Habana harbor. The ship is visible to the Americans as they debark on the main wharf.

"Well, Thomas, 'thar she blows,' so to say."

"Ah, do I call you Ahab then, Captain?" quips Thomas.

"Aye, Ahab it may be. And that rusting whale of a hulk may be my Moby Dick."

"She's not as big as I expected," comments Thomas.

"She's large all right. Don't let appearances deceive you. She's heavy and rides low in the water, made for riverine patrol, not blue water steaming. That's what concerns me!"

"Well, what concerns me, 'sir,' is our dealing with the colonial governor here, Governor Felipe Ginoves de Espinar. I do know that he is only a provisional governor, so he is unlikely to make any major decisions pending his recall to Spain or transfer to other Spanish colonies. I expect he will be no less corrupt than other Spanish officials, so we may have to 'entice' him to return the property which the government in Madrid has already promised to return," remarks Thomas.

"Yes, I've had the privilege of dealing with these Spaniards bastards before, both in Singapura and Manila. On both occasions, I found their officials to be unsavory, to say the least," comments McDougal.

"Unsavory? Corrupt you mean, Captain," interjects Thomas quickly.

"'Corrupt' is not a political word, Thomas. I am surprised at you! Let us just say that, in my experiences, Spanish colonial officials were more concerned about their eventual retirement than the matters at hand. And, of course, part of that retirement equation is just how I could contribute to that eventuality. When they begin telling you about all their needy relatives and expenses, just break to the quick and ask, how much, not how many."

"Yes, I see, sir. Well, we can only do the best we can do. The rest is in the hands of God."

"I'd rather leave God out of the discussion, Thomas. I don't believe that God is much interested in a rusting warship and our petty dealings. Let us save our invocations for the many miles ahead on the open ocean. It is then that we may require the good attentions of the Almighty."

"Are you feeling alright, David, sir?" You are a bit contrary today. It's unlike you."

"Nay, it is very much like me. I'm not partial to the heat, the humidity nor dealing with these damned foreigners. I'm getting myself all worked up inside just imagining it. Let's just get the boat and get the hell out of here."

"Aye-aye, sir. Get the boat and get the hell out of here," mocks Thomas playfully while saluting.

Feet firmly planted on *terra firma*, solid earth, once again, that is the stone wharf jutting into Habana harbor, a civilian-clad David S. McDougal and civilian in fact, Thomas Bayard move with the crowd toward the Customs receiving area. Being two of the few *gringos*, white men, in the crowd, they are soon separated for examination and mild interrogation.

"Why do you come to Cuba, *señor?*" asks a colonial Customs official.

Speaking for them both, McDougal attempts to explain.

"We, my associate and I, are here on official business. I am Captain David S. McDougal, United States Navy, here to take possession of the former Confederate ram, Stonewall, that warship in the harbor." He points toward the ship.

"Ah, then I beg your pardons, *señors*. You must wait here. Someone from the Governor's Office will come for you."

The two are shown a worn, wooden bench long the wall. As the two take their places on the bench a porter brings up their baggage from the ship. Straining to unload one particular box, the porter call to another for assistance, an action which does not go unnoticed by the official.

"What have you there, *señors?* Guns, bullets for *los contras*, the rebels?"

Snapping back, McDougal answers, "No, the ship's money box."

"You mean the Cuban ship in the harbor then, *Señor Capitain?* The money you may leave with me. I will deliver the money to the ship myself."

"No, by God you won't!" barks McDougal.

"Calm yourself, David. Calm yourself. I am sure we come to a reasonable compromise with the Sergeant. Sergeant, is it not, *señor?*"

"*Si*, Sergeant."

"You no doubt have a large family and perhaps a sick mother, *señor* sergeant?"

"Oh, yes, very large and quite sick," repeats the sergeant.

"Very good then, Sergeant, I believe we already have an understanding," finalizes Thomas with a gleam of victory in his eyes. At the very moment of victory for both parties, their bargaining session is disrupted by a representative from the Governor's Office. The sergeant's face melts with disappointment, his catch being snatched away by a far larger predator.

"I am Antonio Suarez, assistant to the Governor, *señors*. Please come with me."

The two are encouraged by the politeness and courtesy extended by *Señor* Suarez as well as having escaped the clutches of the greedy sergeant, his large family and his very sick mother.

"Arrangements have been made for you at La Casa De Oro. Eat, drink and rest. I will come for you again in the morning," explains Suarez.

"Thank you, *Señor* Suarez. You have been most helpful. *Hasta mañana!*"

Evening falls early as McDougal and Bayard seat themselves at a linen and silver set table for supper. A few other guests are scattered about the room, smoking, talking quietly. A spread of *tapas*, Spanish style hors d'oeuvres, is served along with a pitcher of *sangria*, Spanish style red wine mixed with fruit. They eat, drink and comment on the delicious choices before them. Next, assorted island fruits, red beans and rice and grilled reef fish are served. They eat with enthusiasm and are satisfied.

"That was a damn fine meal, Thomas. Not at all what I remember being served in Manila. I'd not wish to go back there. Cuba, so far, suits me better," observes McDougal. "It's been a long and tiring day, Thomas. I think that I shall retire. I'll see you at eight bells. Goodnight."

"Goodnight, sir."

No sooner had McDougal undressed, washed himself with a wet towel and moved toward the bed, there is a quiet knock at the door.

"Yes, who is it?" quickly McDougal grabs his pistol then growls through the door.

His question is answered only by another quiet knock. He, without patience, opens the door. There, standing before him is a young girl, barefoot, wearing a thin, loose dress exposing amble cleavage and long smooth legs.

"*Papito*, papa?" asks the girl.

McDougal stares for a moment, then comprehends her question. *"Do you want to be my daddy?"*

He opens the door widely and, soon, her legs.

Ironclad Ram Warship USS Stonewall

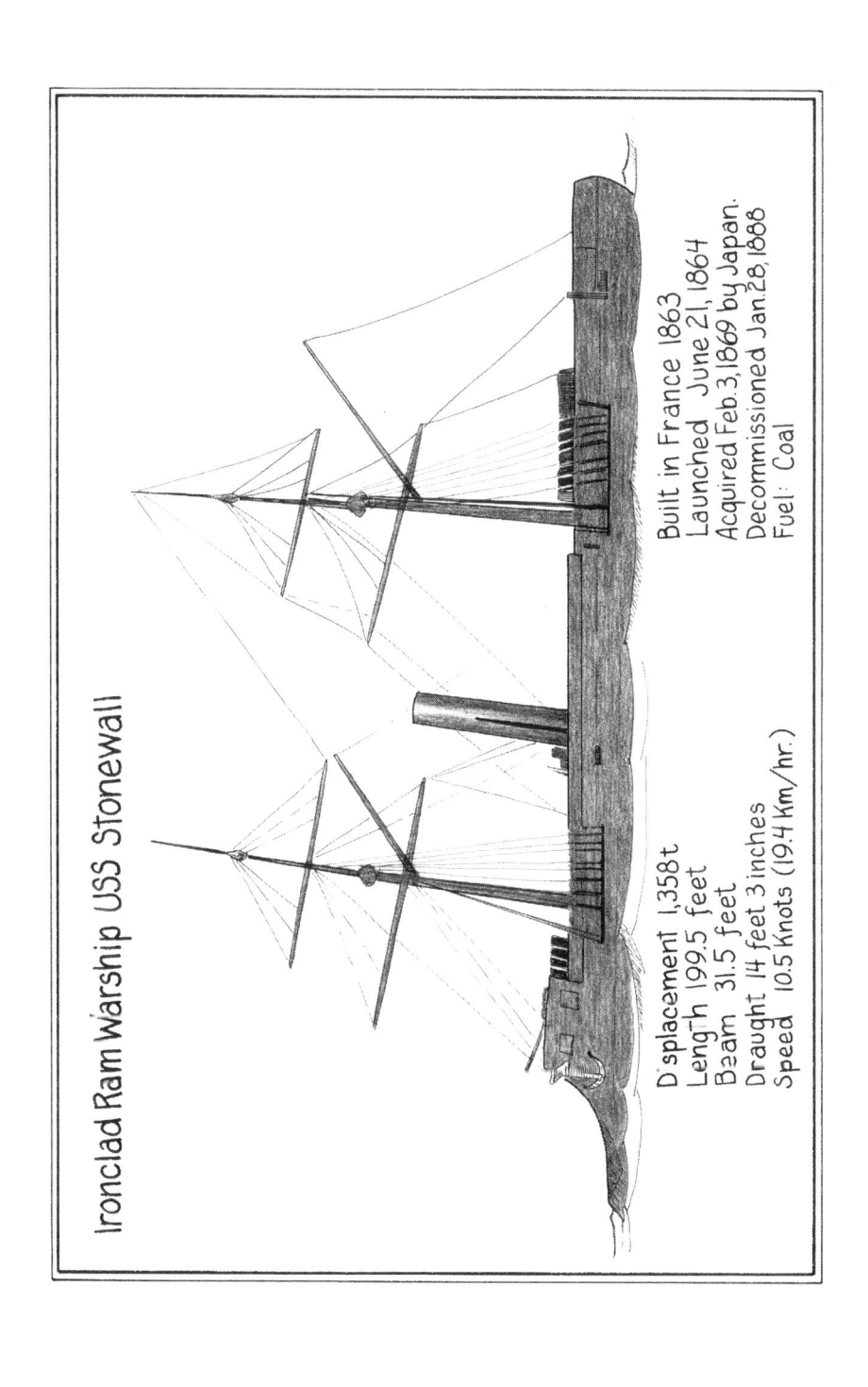

Displacement 1,358 t
Length 199.5 feet
Beam 31.5 feet
Draught 14 feet 3 inches
Speed 10.5 Knots (19.4 km/hr.)

Built in France 1863
Launched June 21, 1864
Acquired Feb. 3, 1869 by Japan.
Decommissioned Jan. 28, 1888
Fuel: Coal

Chapter Eight
The Messenger

Bad joss had descended on the Mori *han*, clan, Hagi castle, and the domain of the Choshu for some years now. The untimely death of Mori Narimoto, the excesses of his son, Mori Takachika, battles with both interventionist and imperial forces, earthquakes, death, woundings, and finally the stigma of defeat. Now, the retainers, court, and common people of the Choshu domain have no one to call lord, no one to lead them good or bad. The limbo of an earthly purgatory hangs over the domain like a cloud of ash after a great conflagration. The burden is made yet heavier post-debacle Lieutenant Goemon, who brought on even further shame in his open defiance of an imperial decree. The clan, retainers and people of the domain are reminded of Goemon's ill-fated misadventure as the bodies of his troop are returned to the castle courtyard, stiff and contorted, in oxcarts. Strangely, Goemon and two others are not among the dead.

From the main guard post of Hagi castle a cyclonic dust cloud rising from beneath the hooves of horse and rider are visible from several *ri* away. Word is passed, first from guard to guard, then throughout the household of an approaching rider. Each of the curious have different and sometimes conflicting emotions as they all wait in anticipation.

The official rider is waved through the main gate. He dismounts, his horse already being led off to water and feed. The rider is then escorted to the great hall on the second floor of Hagi castle. There, waiting expectantly are Counsellor Takahashi and Lady Chizuru, no others. In the hall before the Counsellor and his Lady, the rider knells, then bows ceremoniously. He pushes an ornate, sealed envelope out before him, returning to an upright position in *seiza*, formal Japanese sitting style. The rider, message-bringer, waits while Takahashi carefully opens the envelope and reads the written contents to Lady Chizuru.

```
    His Imperial Highness, Son of Heaven,
extends his greetings and benevolence to
the House of Mori.
    It is at his pleasure and with his
blessing that the Lady Mori Chizuru is
hereby emancipated from the House of Mori
and free to return to her jika, home domin-
ion. Further, under Imperial Protection she
may, at her choosing establish a school of
 "Sisters"  in the name of her so-called
God of the Cross for the purpose of easing
the pain and suffering of subjects of his
Imperial Highness. The hierarchical super-
vision by the Bishop of Rome or his de-
signee is permitted. As it has been
decreed, so it is written.
```

Without the slightest display of emotion, both Takahashi and Lady Chizuru bow to the messenger. Takahashi speaks on her behalf.

"The message from his Imperial Highness is received with gratitude. A formal acknowledgement will be prepared by tomorrow for your return trip. Thank you."

The messenger departs the great hall.

"Am I to believe that which I just heard, Takahashi?" Exclaims Chizuru.

"Yes, my Lady, I suppose you shall, although something does not feel right. I am reluctant to accept the message at face value, but as I have no reason to question an imperial decree, I must. *Omedeto de gozaimasu*, congratulations, my Lady."

"I must prepare at once! Etsuko, tell the others to begin packing. Takahashi and I will make all the necessary notifications and direct that our household goods and supplies be gathered and loaded. We will leave for Shikimi by week's end."

Far to the north, Lieutenant Goemon and his surviving comrades huddle around a small fire near a rivulet in a wooded valley of cedar. Being trained as warriors, not as hunters or gatherers, they find the art of survival exceedingly difficult. As outlaws, they dare not show their faces in village or town lest their presence and location be betrayed. Scattered peasant holdings have little to offer other than pickled vegetables and a little rice. They have yet to uncover hidden *sake*, rice wine or a comely peasant girl. All three wish to return to Hagi castle and take up their previous lives. Unfortunately for them, their return or capture would result in the same swift sentence of death and painful execution.

Desperate and in a dilemma of their own making, Goemon devises a plan to, at least, temporarily mitigate their misery.

"We will move by night, scouting for a residence of quality on the outskirts of a village or hamlet, towns may be garrisoned—too dangerous. We stay hidden during the day, then occupy the place the following evening at mealtime. This will provide us with a good feeding and assure the all the residents are present. The males and the old will be killed at once and disposed of. The females will serve us, feed us and be serviced by us until there is no more to our liking. Then, we will move on in an irregular and unpredictable pattern to the next holding. It is possible for us to live comfortably for months if not longer in this manner. Perhaps we can band together with others of similar position. We need not die today!" outlines Goemon.

"An excellent scheme, Goemon. I can feel a warm cunt wrapped around my cock already," exclaims one of the two.

"Yes, I agree. Let's do it," says the other.

"Good. It is decided then. Let's move," orders Goemon.

Chapter Nine

Diplomacy

The new Ambassador's residence in Tokyo is Yankee built. Beam for beam, board for board, it was designed and erected in Newport R.I., then disassembled and shipped by sea, to be reassembled again on a small patch of "U.S." soil in the new Japanese capital of Tokyo. Ambassador Robert Van Valkenburgh is its first resident and proud of his white, western-style residence-office in the confused assortment of buildings which is Tokyo in late 1868. Tonight Van Valkenburgh welcomes Captain Sugiyama along with Interpreter Ueno to a diplomatic dinner of his own design. Having received official instructions just days before, he is mindful of tonight's purpose. The words of the instructional letter received just days before resonate in his mind.

Hon. Robert Van Valkenburgh

I pray that this letter finds you in good health and conducting fair business on behalf of the United States of America. It is the expressed mission of this Administration to promote Pacific trade with the nations of

Japan and China specifically as well as lessor nations as opportunities may present themselves. To this end, the Grant Administration is making available surplus Army and Navy materials to such friends and allies as could promote our national interests.

The government of Japan has been offered the ex-Confederate ironclad Stonewall for a sum of $500,000 in gold. We are unofficially informed that the offer will be readily accepted. It is expected that your office will provide any and all such support in order to consummate this transaction.

As always, I send my personal best wishes and gratitude for your service

Sincerely,
William Steward, Secretary of State

Van Valkenburgh mumbles to himself. "How could I have nearly fucked this up? A sumptuous dinner, some fine wine, throw in a Cuban cigar or two and the ship will be righted on all fronts.

"Edwards! Let us go over the menu again."

Sitting at a beautiful American walnut table, serviette on his lap, Captain Sugiyama stands and raises his glass in praise of Van Valkenburgh's efforts. Ueno speaks in his stead.

"Mr. Ambassador, a delicious meal. I have never before tasted stuffed pheasant, but after tonight, I shall wish to eat it every Saturday night. The wine, I have had no better, Portugal you say? And the conversation, most enlightening. To you, Mr. Ambassador."

"Thank you, Captain Sugiyama, and to you, Mr. Ueno. I appreciate the sentiment. Shall we retire to the parlor and conduct our business?" proposes Van Valkenburgh.

"Please, after you, Mr. Ambassador."

In deference to the Ambassador, both Ueno and Sugiyama bow as Ueno gestures toward the parlor doorway.

Van Valkenburgh begins. "Now then, gentlemen, I am informed that the subject vessel is available at the stated sum. Acceptance, conveyance and training are to be agreed upon by a certain Captain McDougal and Captain Sugiyama here. This office is to handle payment and other such details as may arise."

"Yes, Ambassador, we agree," begins Sugiyama.

"In principal," clarifies Ueno. "My government would however like to propose a barter, is this the correct word, Mr. Ambassador?"

"Barter, yes, I understand. What kind of barter, Mr. Ueno?" asks Van Valkenburgh suspiciously.

"Goods and services, Mr. Ambassador. We propose a substantial cash payment in gold, pure Japanese *koban*, Tokugawan-era gold pieces, valued at $200,000. The balance of $300,000 plus a bonus ten percent to be paid in future port services, that is; fresh food, water and coal. Our nations enter into a trade-barter arrangement which can be expanded or contracted at mutual convenience and may serve as the basis of bi-lateral trade in the future."

"A complex proposal, so many moving parts. I will need to study the idea," responds VanValkenburgh clearly surprised and having underestimated the prowess of the Japanese. Then, on second thought, Van Valkenburgh says, "Yes, I can see many mutual advantages, Captain Sugiyama. We have several months before the Stonewall—"

Sugiyama interrupts the Ambassador. "Kotetsu, Mr. Ambassador."

"Kotetsu?" questions Van Valkenburgh.

"Yes, Kotetsu. The Imperial Navy warship Kotetsu shall be its name."

"Oh, I see. In any case, we have several months before the 'Kotetsu,' or ex-Confederate Stonewall, arrives here in Japan. Let us expound on the possibilities of your proposal."

The Japanese delegation is pleased at this positive, if tentative response to their proposal, even as Van Valkenburgh mentally examines the personal and profitable angle to such a deal. This, of course, is the same personal and profitable angle that Sugiyama and Ueno have already discussed in partnership and are expecting to exploit in the not too distant future.

Unbeknownst to all gathered in the Ambassador's parlor, their conversations have been overheard by another employed by supporters of the former Tokugawa regime now converging in the northern district of Hokkaido. They too covet the warship Stonewall in order to supplement their seaborne forces currently centered around the Fujiyama, a wooden-hulled, ocean-going, side-wheeler corvette acquired from the American in 1866, a time when they, that is, the Shogunate still reigned.

Chapter Ten
A Great Leap Forward

In late 1868 the government district of Kasumigaseki in Tokyo did not exist as it does today. The Meiji government began however to locate its offices in old samurai residences near Chiyoda castle, the vacated seat of Tokugawan power and expected residence of the Emperor. In this way the government district began to form, the *gaimusho*, Foreign Office, being the first. The "Four" choose, however, to recluse themselves away from the organs of government at Odawara castle, some distance to the south of greater Tokyo. Once a center of fiefdom power during the *sengoku-jidai*, warring states period, Odawara castle lies near the sea and away from the daily doings of the government which they now control.

"Captain Sugiyama and 'our' man Ueno Jiro, that is the Interpreter, have departed Yokohama for the United States. I expect our new warship to arrive within three-four months. Questions?" begins Okubo.

"The Lady Mori Chizuru has renounced her position in the Mori clan. As per the final testament of Mori Takachika, written prior to his *seppuku*, the Choshu domain is forfeit to the Imperial

Throne and his remaining retainers and men-at-arms shall be integrated into the new imperial army and navy."

"The outlaw Goemon is being sought. We expect he is attempting to reach counter-revolutionary forces in the far north. Saigo, do you have anything to add?"

"Yes, Brother Okubo. I have directed Omura to construct a small arms and ammunition manufactory and arsenal here in Tokyo. Initially we have acquired a quantity of small arms from the Prussians. In the near future we will manufacture these ourselves, first by copying the Prussian weapons, then improving upon the design. Larger weapons, canons, ships and such we can negotiate from the American, French or English, other nations have little to offer with the possible exception of the Dutch. Dutch ships are well built."

"And the source of these funds for the purchase of the arms, Saigo?" asks Okubo.

"Ozawa, Brother. As we have previously discussed, activities at the gold mine in Ozawa have been stepped up. This activity as well as our taxation efforts."

"Very good, Brother Saigo."

"And Kido, anything from the Imperial Palace?"

"Just this, Brother. I will keep the Council informed as to the Lady Chizuru's effort with her convent of 'Sisters' in Shikimi. We must make certain that the benevolence of His Imperial Majesty is made known to the *gaijin*. I am seeking a priest of the Cross. Someone we can 'work' with."

"Yes, Brother. Very wise."

"Brothers, we stand on the precipice of a new Japan. Today I envision a great leap forward, but once unleashed, we will have less and less control until the reins of power have passed from we 'Four' to a new and representative government over which we will retain little control. By definition, we will have limited our own usefulness. All this, time will tell.

Chapter Eleven
Tradewinds

Upon the great waters of the Pacific, cutting the swells, paddles slapping the blue-green sea into white froth, black smoke and embers billowing from her stack, the SS Great Republic plows her course from Yokohama toward the golden city of San Francisco. At three hundred-fifty feet long, fifty feet abeam and more than four-thousand tonnes, she is the largest ship of the fleets plying the Pacific commercial trade routes.

Captain Sugiyama and Ueno Jiro are comfortably billeted together in one of the first class cabins on the top-most of her three full decks. On this run she is fully loaded in steerage with Chinese laborers, but the first class cabins are sparsely populated. Captain James Carroll, Master of the SS Great Republic is relieved that he does not have to explain or defend company policy of allowing "Chinamen" onto the upper decks. So far, most of his white, upper-deck gentlemen and occasional accompanying lady have segregated themselves together or remain curious from a discrete distance. Only one or two of the more bigoted white passengers have questioned the company's policy but none have dared to challenge the Captain on this matter.

Food services aboard the SS Great Republic are the pride of the Pacific Mail Steamship Company. With the wind just right, the upper-deck is scented with freshly baked breads, desserts and delights from the ship's bakery. Exotic Asian fruits are offered along with soups and cuts of aged beef, pork and lamb.

Sugiyama and Ueno sit quietly at a corner table in the upper-deck dining room delighted with the cuisine.

Ueno remarks, "What a difference from my first trans-Pacific crossing. Then we slept in 'hanging sacks' and ate only bread and stew. Oh, how Takeshi hated stew. What horrible shits we made."

In spite of the fine dining, Sugiyama, led by Ueno, make their way below now and then to enjoy a simpler fare of rice and vegetables served to the conscript laborers. The fact of their disappearances below deck does not go unnoticed by Captain and crew and is welcomed by a certain Chinese/Japanese passenger slipped aboard in Yokohama and in the pay of the old regime, the Tokugawa Shogunate.

Captain Carroll addresses his Second Mate. "Actually I am somewhat relieved that those uppity Jappers go below once in a while. At least then I don't have to worry about them mingling with our other first class passengers."

Fair weather and a steady eighteen knots make quick work of the passage from Yokohama to San Francisco. No speed records are broken on the twelve-day crossing but the time provided is just enough for the Tokugawa Shogunate payee, Ma Song-il, better known as simply, Ma, to make his observations, prepare his notes and sketch likenesses of each of his targets.

Arriving in San Francisco and before beginning their overland journey east, both Japanese representatives enjoy a few days of active relaxation in the ethnic communities of the city. Ueno learned to play poker aboard the Susquehana years ago, whereas Sugiyama prefers *mahjong*, a game of Chinese origin. Both men game, and win, and lose, then comfort themselves in the arms of one of the many sporting girls floating around the periphery of the games feasting off of both winner and losers alike. Ma keeps loose track of his intended victims, but has arrangements to make elsewhere in the city. Ueno has an ever so slight premonition but shrugs it off as ghosts of days past and loses himself to the scents, music and foods familiar to the Asian nose, ear and palette, as well "companionship on demand" at ten gold dollars a poke.

"Tomorrow we will board the Western Pacific railroad to Sacramento, then continue east through the Sierra Nevada mountains, across a desert, through the mountains again, the Rocky Mountains, and over a vast plain to the great river they call the Mississippi, which bisects this country of theirs. At the river we can find passage on a riverine steamboat which will take us all the way south to Mobile Bay and our new warship, Kotetsu," explains Ueno.

"How long will this journey take us?" asks Sugiyama.

"I am not certain, as much has changed since my last visit here some thirteen years ago. By train, perhaps three or four days, by steamboat, another week. Together I suppose about the same time as it took us to cross from Yokohama to this city. Expect the food to be less palatable, the whiskey more harsh and the ride more rough than our pleasant Pacific cruise," further explains Ueno.

"Is that so? Well, then, I'd best enjoy the softness of another Chinese whore tonight. On second thought, perhaps I'll do two in order to make the night even more memorable," says Sugiyama as he heads toward the door.

In the Elixir Bar at 16th and Guerrero, Ma conducts his business with two recommended men. He pulls out the sketched likenesses.

"These two men are not to complete their trip east. I want no mess, no evidence of murder. They just disappear. Here is our agreed upon payment. Keep what they carry with them, not an unsubstantial amount, I would guess. An equal payment from me will await you here in San Francisco when you provide evidence of the closing. You know where to go, who to ask for. They will examine your evidence and make payment if it is deserved. We will not meet again."

Ma leaves the Elixer bar and is soon aboard the SS China, a sister ship to the SS Great Republic, and on his way to Canton to do his master's work.

The polished wood, etched glass and brass fixtures of the Western Pacific coach are no substitute for the hard, wooden benches and rocky road to Sacramento. The new transcontinental railroad was constructed so rapidly that many sections feature irregularly spaced and rough-cut ties, and little quality ballast to hold tie and rail in place. Sometimes the road grade itself is substandard. Speeds and comfort are reduced accordingly, it will be a long trip. Chinese labor excavated tunnels, which transverse the Sierra Nevada Mountains, are engineering marvels as are the cuts, fills, trestles and bridges spanning chasm and canyon. The scenery is truly spectacular, but this only partially mitigates the boredom and discomfort of the trip.

Ueno remarks, "Sugiyama, you appear to be even more uncomfortable than I."

"Were I truly to confess the burning and dripping of my manhood, I would then have to further confess a certain foreboding I had during the 'act.' I should have taken the time to seek out a nice Japanese girl rather than satisfying myself with the first two Koreans proffered me," laments Sugiyama.

"Garlic eaters? How could you stand the smell?" asks a somewhat surprised Ueno.

"My efforts weren't focused on their heads! My carnal interests led me elsewhere, thus my current predicament. I wonder how these *gaijin* deal with sicknesses of one's manhood. *Kuso*, shit, it hurts to pass water!"

"These Koreans were offered to you?"

"Yes, recommended by a frontier-looking man."

"A white man offered you the Koreans?"

"Yes. That is strange, isn't it? I wasn't thinking clearly with the whiskey and my desire to fuck as much as possible last night," reflects Sugiyama. "This must be his idea of a joke."

"A joke would be the best outcome I can think of. Keep your eyes open for your frontiersman. If you see him again, it could be that we have been followed."

Chapter Twelve
Preparations

Having foiled the Customs sergeant at his own game, McDougal and Bayard are expecting a higher level of play with Governor Espinar.

The next morning at their meeting in the once magnificent Governor's mansion, they are beyond surprise when the meeting is swiftly concluded at the cost of only a small port and maintenance fee in addition to the amount previously negotiated by the respective governments. It seems Governor Espinar is more than happy to reduce one of his high profile responsibilities given the current nativist insurrection and other troubles plaguing the old Spanish colony. Further, he desires no extended negotiation or trouble with the Americans.

They depart the Governor's mansion and are soon ferried out to the ex CSS Stonewall at anchor in the bay. Climbing aboard, the two Spanish guards dismiss themselves and embark the returning ferry. The ex-CSS Stonewall is now occupied property of the United States of America. Captain McDougal pulls a tightly wrapped package out of his seabag.

"What's that?" questions Bayard.

As McDougal answers, he is already making his way toward the fantail of the ship. "Our colors, Bayard, our colors!"

The unfurling Stars and Stripes catch the slight breeze moving across Habana harbor. For the moment McDougal is satisfied, but soon turns to Bayard and begins issuing orders to his one-man crew.

"This is our post until relieved, Bayard. Find yourself a cabin, any cabin but mine. Then bring a piece of paper and a pencil, and we shall allocate tasks accordingly. With luck, the temporary crew will arrive within days."

"Aye, sir," responds Bayard more tongue in cheek than seriously and scurries off to find the second-best cabin on the ship.

McDougal purposefully mentally allocates tasks as he sets out on a tour of his new command.

"Check the integrity of hull. Check the pumps. Check the condition of the boilers and the contents of the coal bunkers. Make note of the bearings, shaft and seal. I'll send Bayard off to deal with the Cubans for water, grub and coal," mumbles McDougal to himself as he methodically crisscrosses the ship.

Within a fortnight, a skeleton crew of sailors gleaned from three transiting American naval vessels fill out McDougal's roster. Looking more rust than ready, he gives the order for her two boilers to be lit.

"Fire the boilers, Mr. Edwards."

The boiler room is a narrow confines located between the coal bunkers and armor plating for protection. The design intention was for the boilers to be placed below the waterline as shelter against incoming missiles and for the coal to be gravity fed for maximum efficiency. Unfortunate for the engineering crew, in the end, the design is changed, her spaces cramped, inefficient and of course, hot.

"Attaining minimum pressure for propulsion, sir!" yells engineering officer Lieutenant Edwards into the Gosmer tube.

"Double check all pipes and fittings, Mister Edwards. Then give me minimum revolutions and double check the integrity of the shaft, seals and bearings. Make certain everything is over-lubricated. I'll not criticize you for a little grease, Edwards."

"Very good, sir. Everything that moves will be lathered in lubricant," replies Edwards with a smile.

"We'll polish the rust off slowly, Mister Edwards." Now using a voice trumpet, McDougal continues his litany of commands. "Raise the anchors three feet off the bottom, we'll let 'em drag. Be prepared to drop them again on command."

And it is in this manner that Captain McDougal and his new crew prepare and test the Stonewall for departure onto the open sea and direct Mobile Bay.

By design, the one-hundred-eighty-seven-foot vessel was to attain thirteen knots sustained, but a deeper draught and ill-fitted iron armor limits her speed to just over ten knots. Captain McDougal plans for just seven knots at sea, desiring to "go easy" on the already corroded French machinery.

Captain McDougal tests the rudder for free and full range of motion. "Mister Edwards, does the rudder pivot properly? Do the rudder chains appear intact and well fastened? She seems to respond correctly to wheel inputs, but we won't know for certain until we get underway."

"She appears to be sound, sir," replies Edwards.

"Very good then. Mister Edwards, all ahead slow. We'll cruise about the harbor like tourists. The first such shakedown in naval history, I imagine. Quartermaster, take the wheel, ahead slow, just enough for steerage. Roughly follow the contours of the harbor and return to this position. Proceed," commands McDougal.

Thomas Bayard at his side as if an Aide de Camp, McDougal takes his place on the bridge to observe Habana from the point of view of the harbor as the ship moves in its circuit from Atares Bay to Marimelena Bay, to Guanabacoa Bay and back to Atares again.

"Excellent. Drop anchor. Secure the ship. We depart at six bells tomorrow morning. First Officer, no shore leave tonight, but a ration of rum for the crew will do nicely," orders McDougal.

McDougal turns toward Bayard and winks. "When in Rome, Thomas."

"Secure the ship, no shore leave, ration of rum. Very good, sir," repeats the First Officer.

"I will retire to my quarters. If you have questions, please do not hesitate to ask, Mister. Till six bells then. Goodnight."

"Goodnight, Captain."

"Bayard, you may join me for a celebratory nightcap or retire, your choice."

"A nightcap it shall be, Captain."

As per Captain McDougal's schedule, the French built, English armed, ex-Confederate, now American, soon-to-be Japanese warship clears Habana harbor at 0630 the next day on a clear morning. She enters into the Atlantic, turning northwest toward the Gulf of Mexico and Mobile Bay. McDougal's final, circuitous voyage to the Japans begins.

Chapter Thirteen

The elation of departure soon dissipates as the oxcarts grind slowly southward from Hagi castle to the fishing village of Shimonoseki. Etsuko reaches out to mark a wheel spoke, then counts the seconds it takes for the wheel to slowly turn one revolution. But with each laborious tug of the ox, the tight group of mistress and handmaidens is one step closer to Shikimi and their new life.

In front of the carts ride a small group of mounted men at arms, one of which carries an imperial banner. To the rear, another group of equal size, all to insure the safe and unquestioned passage of ex-Lady, now Prioress Agnes and her ex-handmaidens, now Sisters of Charity of the God of the Cross.

Nothing escapes Chizuru's attention. She is cheered by the beauty of the pristine rural landscapes, makes note of landmarks and registers the facial expressions of her escort glancing lustfully at her ladies sitting awkwardly in the carts.

As they approach the village of Shimonoseki, where they will embark small boats in order to cross over the Shimonoseki Straits, Chizuru is unhappy that the escort of "Mori" men will not be relieved and changed on the other side. She does not really trust these men in spite of the imperial banner under which they ride. These are still "Mori" men. Their eyes express indifference, lust, even hate toward her and her ladies.

Chizuru speaks quietly to Etsuko. "Look, the trenches and bunkers are all but empty. Only a few rusted canons remain in place. Those guns are too antique to have any practical military value except for the iron they are made of. The Mori banner no longer flutters above the blockhouses. I do not know whether I am cheered or saddened by the change."

"Nothing has really changed, my Lady," begins Etsuko.

"Don't call me that! I am your sister now. Call me Sister Agnes or Elder Sister, whichever you feel comfortable with," corrects Chizuru.

"Pardon me, Elder Sister. Nothing has physically changed here, only the printed, silk banners have changed, but Elder Sister, the place is full of ghosts. I can feel them. Why am I suddenly afraid?"

"It is a disturbed site, Etsuko. Men died needlessly here. Men inspired by power, greed and evil on both sides. Let us pray to help sanctify this place."

The Sisters pray. *"O Creator of all that is visible and invisible. Place your hand upon these waters, upon the land. Calm the restless spirits with your presence. Come, be with us in this place. Let it be."*

After prayer, the Sisters embark the small boats. The boats, heavy with luggage and passengers tack their way across the narrow and treacherous Straits under leaden skies. Etsuko reaches out, feeling the cold waters run through her fingers, day-dreaming of a life of without a master or mistress, a life of equals, a life devoted to God and to good.

Etsuko senses only a slight nudge, but the nudge is enough to make her lose her balance and fall into the cold waters of the

Inland Sea. Wrapped in tight layers of kimono silk, swimming is not possible even if she had known how to swim. After a few panicked moments she slips beneath the surface and joins so many others killed or drowned in this very place. The angry ghosts are suddenly calmed with the presence of such pure innocence in their midst.

"Save her, save her!" screams Chizuru.

"It is already too late, my Lady. She is gone. The kimono, the cold waters and the current, they pulled her down quickly. There was no saving her," replies one of the guards as matter-of-factly.

Chizuru speaks loud enough to be heard by all. "I know that you despise us. And I also know that this was no accident. Etsuko was a kind and loving girl. Why her? Why not me?" cries Chizuru.

One of the men at arms, with a smirk on his face, replies, "Because you are our Lady."

Far to the north, some *ri* south of the town of Akita, Goemon and his two comrades have decided on a target residence. It is a rather large two and one half story structure with a glazed blue tile roof. It sits isolated with its outbuildings, surrounded by flooded rice fields. There is only one light road in and out.

One of Lieutenant Goemon's comrades speaks out. "I am concerned, Goemon. This place is too nice. A retired government official or *bushi* may live there."

"If he is retired, then we shall retire him further. If he be an official, then he can officiate in the hereafter. In either case, we will enjoy the fruits of his labors as well as any grieving lovelies which he may have left behind."

Goemon and his fugitive comrades inhale the sweet scent of braised meat emanating from the target residence. Their hungry mouths water involuntarily, their stomachs growl. They have not really eaten in several days. At dusk, Goemon and one other move with stealth along either side of the light road toward the main building. The third of their party remains concealed at a distance ready to cut down any one who may try to flee or unfortunates coming to call.

Goemon slides open the front door with suddenness leaving everyone sitting at meal startled. He growls. "Don't move. Don't cry out. Try to flee and you will die where you stand."

There are seven seated around a glowing brazier. Some grilling meat and vegetables begin to burn.

"You there! Continue to cook all that you have. We are hungry," commands Goemon.

The *pater familia*, head of the household, glares at Goemon, for he knows what he is. Goemon points at the man and his teenage son and says, "You two, stand up, move outside. Nobu-*kun*, honorific familiar, you watch these others. And don't fuck anyone until I come back!"

"Oh, so you want to watch, eh," jokes Nobu.

Goemon herds the two men outside, then contrary to plan, into the family *kura*, storehouse and locks the door. True, he is a fugitive, but he is still *bushi*. He will not have the blood of innocents on his hands. After the door of the *kura* is secure and locked, Goemon moves into the open and waves the third man in. Once back in the house, Goemon and Nobu wait for their comrade while snacking on the meal and sizing up their take. Nobu points to the youngest of the females.

"I'll take her for now. You and Yoshi can split the remaining four between you."

"No, I'll take the young one. You and Yoshi take the others. But first, eat," states Goemon with finality.

They feast without talking. They drink without breathing, all while staring at the females now huddled together against the wall. Goemon is the first to finish eating.

"You, girl, come!" He pushes her into an adjacent room as he removes his trousers and pulls aside his *fundoshi*, Japanese-style loincloth. "Now suck and stroke." As awkward and inexperienced as she is, he soon ejaculates into her mouth. "Again!" he commands.

When he is finished with her, he leads her outside and locks her up with her father and brother in the storehouse. Behind her tears and humiliation she is grateful that he has spared her virginity. She thanks her gods profusely.

Nobu and Yoshi are thoroughly enjoying the feelings of a full stomach, the glow of sake and being sandwiched between two women each, even if they aren't quite as young and smooth-skinned as Goemon's take. Having both spilled themselves more than once they fall fast asleep within the folds of their temporary wives. The youngest and strongest of those ravaged is the eldest daughter of the family come home for a visit. The three fugitives have paid no notice of the baby sleeping peacefully nearby. The young mother did not take down her hair during the brutal sexual frolic, rather left it up, secured with comb and pin which is the fashion of the day. Slowly, she rises to her knees, remaining naked, should her abuser stir, she will simply mount him again as if nothing were amiss. The other three victims watch as Yoko pulls one of the eighteen-inch-long *kanzashi* pins from her hair bun behind her head. She crouches, carefully takes aim, then drives the pin up the nose and into the brain of her assailant, sleeping Nobu. He utters a soft grunt and dies instantly. With unspoken understanding and consent, Yoko grabs garment, sandal and her child and silently disappears out the door and into the night. She knows nothing of her father, brother and little sister locked in the storehouse.

Sometime later before dawn, Goemon is harshly awakened by a hard kick to his ribs. Instinctfully he reaches for his *katana*, but it is gone. Three men stand over him. Yoko has returned from the village with the local magistrate and men at arms. The magistrate speaks.

"You, on your feet!"

"Nobu!" calls Goemon, but there is no answer.

"Was that his name? What about the other? In any event, it doesn't matter. Your associates have gone to be with the gods, if they ever revered any. But don't worry. You will join them soon. Take him away!"

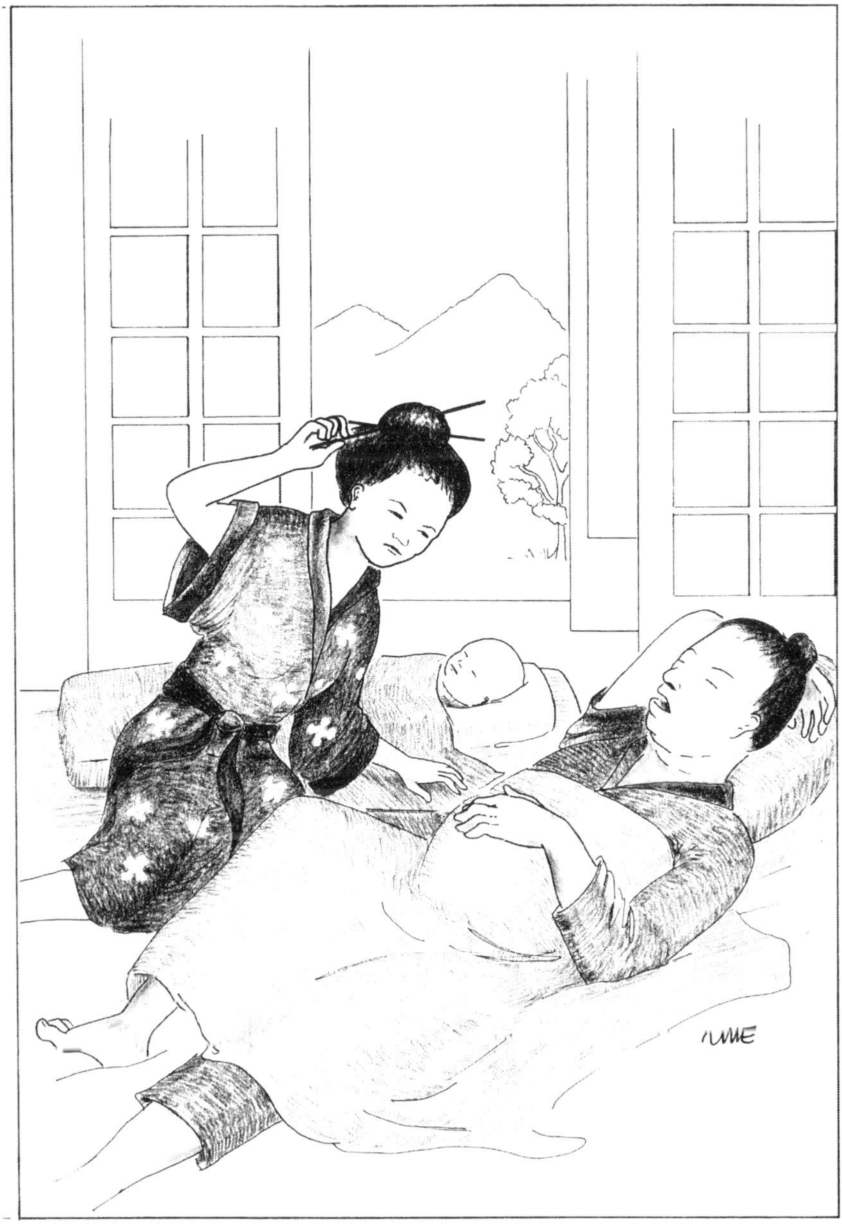

Chapter Fourteen
The Dilemma

Captain Sugiyama and Ueno Jiro had departed for the United States only several days before when Ambassador Van Valkenburgh is approached at a local eatery by a rather polished fellow with a slight English accent. Pleasantries are exchanged and soon they find themselves lunching and drinking together, discussing any number of worldly matters over which the young stranger has a commanding knowledge. Van Valkenburgh is impressed, which, of course, is the point. The young man introduces himself as John Barbour, sets down his drink and looks Van Valkenburgh straight in the eye.

"Let me be perfectly honest with you, Mister Ambassador, our meeting today is not by chance. I have been planning to introduce myself for some time now, but this matter can wait no longer," confides the young man.

"I see. Then you are not who you say you are," replies Van Valkenburgh icily.

"On the contrary, Mr. Ambassador, I am exactly who I say I am. I am an English-educated, American-born, citizen of the world, beholden to no country, travelling without restraint around this vast globe. As you can imagine, my travels, my tastes, my needs are not inexpensive. To this end, I occasionally perform an odd job for a client or two.

"You are an assassin then?" squeaks Van Valkenburgh, eyes darting, seeking a place an avenue of escape.

"Assassin? No, nothing so crude as that. In any case, why would anyone seek to harm you, Mr. Ambassador?"

"Why, I don't know. The world is a dangerous place."

"I simply wish to make you an offer on behalf of my employer."

"An offer?"

"Yes, an offer. A scheme which will provide for you in your retirement and cause no loss of equilibrium in the world."

"You speak in riddles. Can you not simply state your business for my consideration? I warn you, however, do not try to trick me. I am an intelligent man," whines Van Valkenburgh already clearly out of his league.

"Very intelligent, Mr. Ambassador, and a close personal friend of Secretary William Steward, I understand."

"Yes, this is true. How do you know these things?"

"I know many things, Robert. May I call you Robert?"

"I do not care what you call me, just state your business! Someone might see us."

"See what? Two well-dressed Caucasian men discussing matters of consequence over lunch? I represent the legitimate government of Japan, the Tokugawa Shogunate."

"But the Shogun is gone. The Emperor Meiji and the Oligarchy govern Japan."

"That is what 'they' would like you to think. The Tokugawa are not gone, simply temporarily displaced by an illegal *coup d'état* orchestrated by clans which surround the Emperor and deceive him with promises and slogans. Did you realize, Robert, that the Shogun is married to the Emperor's sister? My employer, supporters of the Shogunate, has shown great interest in the warship being offered to the Oligarchy. We have other vessels of course, many other vessels. The Kaiten and the powerful Fujiyama, a corvette given to the Shogunate by your own government only two years ago are just two examples. We wish to supplement Kaiten and Fujiyama with the Stonewall. With such ships at our disposal we can confidently challenge the Oligarchy here and on their home turf along the Inland Sea."

"What can I possibly do?" questions Van Valkenburgh.

"You can help stop the sale of the warship to the Oligarchy. Tender the Shogunate's point of view to your government, that is; that the Shogunate remains the legal government of Japan. The Oligarchy represents rebels and malcontents, intent by the way of expelling all foreigners. Have you not heard of the *Sonno Joi* movement?"

"*Sonno Joi?*"

"Yes, *Sonno Joi*—Revere the Emperor, expel the barbarians. This is the slogan which brought the Oligarchy to power."

"Oh, my God, we have been deceived into supporting the wrong side," gasps Van Valkenburgh.

"My point exactly, Mr. Ambassador."

"We can count on you then? Count on you when it matters?"

"Yes, I suppose you can. I will write a letter to Secretary Steward forthwith. I'll request that he enjoin the sale of the Stonewall to the Meiji government and stop Captain Sugiyama and Interpreter Ueno until this matter can be more thoroughly reviewed. This is what I can do."

"Oh, I wouldn't worry about them. The Captain and his man may never reach their destination anyway. One of my men shadow them now."

"You will have them murdered then?"

"Oh, Robert, you are so melodramatic. They will simply disappear somewhere in that vast wild west of yours. But the Oligarchy has other men. So do your part in assisting us in having the warship sale offer withdrawn. Do this and you will be handsomely rewarded. Betray us and, well, let me just add, do not betray us!"

Van Valkenburgh continues to sit for a moment, silently and in a mild state of shock. "Counter-revolutionary murderers. Debonair, smooth-talking assassins. I identified him and his kind correctly the first time. But what can I do? First, I'll send Mrs. Van Valkenburgh and the children home on leave. Second, I will write Secretary Steward and request a Marine guard be established to protect the embassy from a non-specific threat, no, better yet, in this 'turmultuous' times. This John Barbour, if that really is his name, will not know the actual contents of my letter. Then I'll just wait for events to unfold and make certain that the eventual victors are assured of our and my confidence and support. Yes, this is how I shall play my hand. A letter, a letter to the Secretary."

Hon. Secretary William Steward

Greetings to you, Mr. Secretary. I hope this letter finds you in good health.

Somewhat contrary to the reported stability here in the Japanese capitol, it has come to our attention that there exists unspecified threats to the recently established Meiji government and possibly to the western diplomatic community. As instructed, this Embassy has strictly adhered to a policy of non-interference; however, we believe it to be prudent to take certain steps to safeguard American lives and property.

To this end, I request that a Marine guard be temporarily attached to the Embassy for this purpose. Once said threat dissipates, as I am certain it will, the guard could be withdrawn. I hope that you will agree to this relatively minor and prudent course of action and will allow a speedy implementation of this request.

As always, my warmest regards.
Robert Van Valkenburgh, Ambassador

Chapter Fifteen
A Seat at the Table

Seated like four judges behind a cloth covered table in the great hall of Odawara castle, the Oligarchy prepare for their next audience, an audience of one.

Okubo gestures, then commands, "bring in Father Paul." For his "Brother's" benefit Okubo expounds. "Father Paul is of the French Foreign Missions Society. Historically, these Society missionaries have demonstrated enthusiasm only toward their missions and have not meddled in local politics. Let us examine this one and see just how far he is willing to bend for the sake of his Order, his Church and his God."

A slight and mild-mannered man enters the hall, bows and proceeds forward to where a chair has been provided for him.

"Please sit," says Kido in a business-like manner. "Father Paul of the Foreign Missions Society, is it?" asks Kido.

"Yes, your honor, I am he."

"You have been requested here through the good offices of your embassy. You are French then?"

"I am first a servant of God, your honor. But as you refer to the place of my birth, I hail from Rocheguide, a small village near the old Roman garrison town of Orange in the Rhone valley. Later, I was sent and educated in Alsace, the town of Saarbrucken on the frontier between German and French-speaking peoples. I am comfortable in either culture or language," explains Father Paul as matter-of-factly.

"And so you are. Comfortable in conversational English as well, I see."

"The English, though few in numbers, have made their language the de facto tongue of business and commerce throughout the world. In order to effectively spread the Good News of God, it requires a knowledge of many secular things."

"You must be quite effective in your ministry then, Father Paul," goads Kido.

"I am but a humble servant. If my efforts have borne any fruit, then it is only to the greater glory of God."

"I see," says Kido beginning to show impatience with his overly humble man and his verbal jousting.

Okubo tacks back from Kido's line of questioning.

"Father Paul, the government of Japan, at the behest of his Imperial Highness, wishes to make a gesture of sincerity to the growing diplomatic community here in Tokyo. To this end, we are prepared to allow the establishment of a church, a Catholic church, in the Tsukiji Teppozu district of the city. Does this gesture of interest to you, Father Paul?" asks Okubo knowingly.

"Yes, of course. I simply was not expecting such a magnanimous gesture," responds Father Paul clearly taken by surprise.

"Naturally we would expect your flock to be primarily diplomats and their families, but western businessmen, sailors even

Japanese citizens may freely attend," continues Okubo further baiting his trap.

"Japanese citizens? I am allowed to announce God's Good News to your people?" asks Father Paul incredulously.

"You are to be so allowed. We do have one request, however."

"A request?"

"Yes, a simple request. On the island of Kyushu, near the village of Shikimi, there is a noble lady with several others requesting spiritual guidance from a leader of their faith."

Father Paul, clearly shocked by this revelation interrupts. "You are saying that there are Japanese Christians, Catholics in Kyushu?"

"There were once many so-called Christians in Japan. It is unfortunate that those people chose to deny the divinity of their Emperor and follow misguided leaders. Truly, difficult and regrettable days, but that was many years ago. Today we talk about the future of Japan. It is an arduous journey by land to reach the village of which I speak, but by sea only several days. We request that you include the Lady Chizuru and her followers into your small flock. Visit them, minister to their needs. From time to time we will ask you of their progress."

"Spy on them. You wish me to spy upon my own flock?"

"On the contrary, Lady Chizuru has disassociated herself from politics. She is not interested in matters of this world, only in those of her god. His Imperial Majesty has taken an interest in her well-being, and we merely wish to have measure of her progress. Are you willing to bear this additional burden?" asks Okubo emotionlessly.

"My Lord's burden is light. I carry it happily."

"Then we are in agreement, Father Paul. You may go for now. You can expect to hear from us from time to time."

Okubo relaxes slightly as Father Paul departs. He turns and addresses the others.

"Brothers, the die is cast. The western powers argue amongst themselves and fight for a scraps at our table. We feign interest in their literature and culture, but really seek only their technologies. We lull them into submission with the slightest concessions to their god. They seek to carve us up like China. But it is we who will carve them away from their colonial possessions in Asia and it is we who will have been invited to a seat at their table, the table of nations."

Chapter Sixteen
Kotetsu

Ma's men watch their unsuspecting prey mile after railroad mile. Men of habit themselves, they watch to establish patterns and weaknesses which may be turned to their advantage at the moment of truth.

Zack, the self-appointed leader of the two murder-for-hire men, has concluded that the most advantageous moment could be when either of the, would be, victims use the privy to the rear of the railroad coach during the hours of darkness. Zack plans with Matt in hushed voices.

"After dark, along any secluded stretch of track, I will follow one of the Jappers back to the privy. You stay and watch the other. We'll let him have his last piss or shit, then when he shows his slope-headed face, I'll gut 'em like a trout, fleece 'em and throw what's left off the train to the varmints."

"Good plan, Zack, but what about the other one?" questions Matt.

"Same goes for the second Japper. When he goes back to look after his friend, we'll dispatch 'em to hell also, so that'nd they don't get lonesome. That will give us plenty of time to check their personals for anything of value. Then, we simply get off at the next stop and catch the next train back to San Francisco. No one will miss the Jappers for many days. By that time, the varmits will have had their feast and fill, and we'll be hundreds of miles away. We collect the second half of our pay, maybe spend a little time south of the border with a *senorita*, sweetheart, or two until our money runs out," outlines Zack, his lips already sipping a frothy *cerveza*, beer, and enjoying the affections of a comely *senorita* of his dreams.

That evening, as per Zack's plan, Sugiyama leaves his seat next to Ueno and moves swayingly, bench by bench, back toward the privy. Sugiyama, *bushi*, samurai, by birth and training, senses the man following him. He enters the dark privy as if he suspects nothing. While sitting, Sugiyama pushes forward a centuries-old *tanto*, Japanese short sword, tucked into his sleeve.

He waits. Zack shows his impatience by losing focus. When the coach hits cross-tracks and begins to rock, Sugiyama opens the privy door. Mentally and physically in a state of readiness, he easily parries Zack's clumsy knife thrust and counters with an upward slash across the cowboy's throat severing everything save the bone in his neck. Cowboy, would-be murderer, Zack falls at Sugiyama's feet in a heap. Sugiyama steps over the bloody pile and returns to his seat unperturbed. Sugiyama speaks not a word of the incident to Ueno. He waits and observes all around. The anxiety-filled Matt soon shows he cards as he bolts for the back of the coach. Stopping only long enough at the prostrate, bloodied body of his criminal partner in order to clean-out his pockets and grab his gun, Matt moves to the rear of the train, jumps into the darkness and is gone. The murder for hire men simply disappear.

Unaware of the scheme to delay the Meiji government's procurement of the Kotetsu, Sugiyama and Ueno do begin to piece together the Tokugawa plot. With the American murder for hire men dead or fled, and Ma happily en route to Canton, the window for disruption of the transfer has closed. Ma will, by the change of fortunes, soon find himself without employment and the Tokugawa find themselves without a ship, and probably without hope of turning the Meiji tide back into their favor.

At the Union Pacific depot in Council Bluffs, Iowa, Captain Sugiyama and Ueno Jiro disembark this third of three trains and seek riverine transport for their journey south on the Mississippi River and on to Mobile Bay. Luckily, the two find The Dubuque, a new side-wheeler of the Keokuk Northern Line accepting passengers for all points south. The Council Bluffs agent for the Keokuk Northern Line had never seen an Asiatic man before and assumed Sugiyama and Ueno to be Indians.

"No Injuns allowed in First Class!" he firmly states.

Ueno, having experienced Caucasian prejudices many times before, but also aware of the sometimes fatal consequences of misunderstandings, is slow to react. He nods, acknowledges the ticket agent's statement, then pulls from his pouch a carefully folder letter, with the printed

letterhead of the Secretary of State of the United States of America. He offers the letter to the suspicious agent without a word being spoken.

Office of the Secretary of State

To whom it may concern: Know ye that the bearers of this document are guests of the United States Gov-

ernment and are to be accorded any and all such courtesies and privileges due to officially invited guests. Extend to the bearer(s) all possible assistance. Should further clarification be required, please present this document to the nearest federal authority, military or civilian.

William Steward, Secretary

At the time of Reconstruction there still existed federal occupation and scattered zones of marital law, therefore compliance to a federal request was not always automatic or a matter of fact. Fortunately for Sugiyama and Ueno, Council Bluffs, Iowa is a strongly unionist town and the ticket agent for the Keokuk Northern Line a pro-union man, so the requested tickets are soon provided. A day later, Sugiyama and Ueno continue their journey south, sightseeing at the slow pace of the Mississippi current courtesy of the Keokuk Northern Line and its newest riverine side-wheeler, the Dubuque. The cruise south provides the two with a relaxing respite; they eat, they drink, they gamble, all while viewing the passing wonders of America's river culture and scenery.

Approaching New Orleans, however, Ueno, usually reserved by nature, experiences a wellspring of mixed emotions. He finds himself saddened at the end of a carefree and wonder- filled cruise down one of the great rivers of the world. Yet, there remains within him the trauma of manslaughter committed before his eyes, when Okada, his comrade on his first visit to America, was killed in a racially charged incident in front of a Bourbon Street bar. And finally, he feels a confirmation of his own worth at being chosen not once but twice to represent his country by two consecutive governments in the midst of revolution.

From the piers of New Orleans, they continue on by boarding another vessel to Mobile Bay where the object of their mission sits tethered to a wharf awaiting its distinguished guests and proxy new owners.

On the morning of their boarding the Kotetsu, Ueno is surprised by Captain Sugiyama emerging from his hotel room resplendent in his new uniform, that of a Senior Captain in the new Japanese Imperial Navy. In the few years since Ueno's first acquaintance with Sugiyama, he has evolved from a forgotten Tokugawan Lieutenant Commander, "the ship counter of Yokohama" to a Senior Captain and Master to be of the Imperial Navy's first steam-powered, ironclad warship.

With evident confidence, Captain Sugiyama, followed closely by "Interpreter" Ueno Jiro walks briskly along the wharf toward the vessel. Mounting the gangplank, Captain Sugiyama stops short of the quarterdeck, turns sharply toward the U.S. National Ensign flying off the fantail of the ship and salutes. Having unexpectedly performed this respect and courtesy, he then turns to the Officer of the Deck and speaks in loud and commanding voice. "Captain Yohei Sugiyama, Imperial Japanese Navy requesting permission to come aboard."

The Officer of the Deck, not yet having recovered from the surprise of Sugiyama's masterful performance replies automatically. "Permission granted." Captain Sugiyama has finally come into his own.

Chapter Seventeen
The Menagerie

Webster defines a "menagerie" as "a collection of wild animals kept especially to be shown to the public." In McDougal's estimation he has been handed a menagerie of characters, all caged up in a somewhat exotic relic of a ship, he simply refers to as "The Beast."

The odd-looking Stonewall is one hundred eighty-seven feet in length, displacing one thousand-five hundred tonnes, significantly smaller than the SS Great Republic which ferried Sugiyama and Ueno across the Pacific. Her two French built, double-reciprocating steam engines produce twelve hundred horsepower driving two shaft-connected propellers. Due to design flaws and miscalculations, she carries insufficient reserves of coal and is rather slow. If pressed, one can conserve coal by cruising on one boiler and/or revert to sailing, as she has two masts and carries ample canvas.

Having made the transit from Habana to Mobile Bay, McDougal is confident he can nurse the vessel all the way to Japan. He pens a letter to Secretary Welles.

Hon. Gideon Welles, Secretary of the Navy

Sir,

 Pursuant to your directive, the subject ex-CSS Stonewall ironclad has successfully been repatriated to Port Mobile Bay, United States of America We experienced no appreciable problems in transit. For the transit to Japan, a veteran crew has already reported aboard and is familiarizing itself with the vessel. Ex-Confederate Master, Captain T.J. Page has also reported aboard as have the representatives of the Japanese government today.
 Somewhat to my surprise, the Japanese representatives consist of a Senior Naval Captain and his interpreter. As I was expecting civilian representatives of the Japanese government, I pray that this does not cause any confusion in the chain of command, I am confident it will not.
 The vessel is well supplied and ready. I plan to depart on the morrow. I will endeavor to keep your office informed as to our progress as far as this is possible given the remoteness of some of our scheduled ports of call.
 Thank you for bestowing upon me the honor of representing our country with this unique command. I look forward to a full accounting of the voyage with you upon our return.

Your servant
David S. McDougal, Captain

Captain McDougal has retained Lieutenant Edwards as Engineering Officer. Given the uniqueness of the mission, ship and crew, McDougal has named Bayard, technically a civilian, as Second Officer, given his naval record and wartime experience. Ex-Confederate Naval Captain T.J. Page is named as First Officer. Captain Sugiyama and Interpreter Ueno are not designated in the chain of command but are allowed free and unfettered access throughout the ship subject only to orders from the Officer of the Deck or the Captain himself.

Captain McDougal, correspondence complete, puts down his pen and calls for the Officer of the Deck.

"Have this message taken ashore and sent as a telegram immediately. Second, schedule an officer's call for eight bells this evening. Thank you. That is all."

Seated around a table in the captain's cabin, which will serve as the officer's wardroom, McDougal outlines their mission and voyage to Tokyo Bay, Japan.

"Good evening, gentlemen. Tomorrow morning at six bells we will embark on an historical mission. We will get underway to points south, the Magellan Straits, the west coast of South America, the Sandwich Islands and finally Japan. It will not be a quick and easy transit, as we are limited in coal reserves as well as speed given the, shall I say, uniqueness of this vessel. I am planning for a steady seven knots on average. Contrary or prevailing winds, storms and such may slightly alter our forward progress.

"Let me be frank you regarding the distances involved. It is roughly ten thousand nautical miles around the South American continent, that is, once we depart Port of Spain, which is fifteen hundred miles south of where are moored presently.

"It is a further four thousand miles from northern Ecuador to the Sandwich Islands, a tropical port of call at which, at least, the crew have great expectations. Finally, another four thousand miles to our destination in Japan. All told, we have about twenty thousand nautical miles in which to become better acquainted. If we average the seven and one half knots I have planned, then it means one hundred-eleven plus days cruising in addition to time in ports of call for coaling and resupply.

"Given favorable winds, we will spread the sheets in order to conserve coal. We will experiment with different steam power configurations with and without canvas in order to improve speed and reduce coal consumption. Departmental questions can be addressed in due course. Are there any general questions?"

Bayard breaks the general silence around the table. "Well, we'll all best be on our good behavior then," quips Bayard light-heartedly.

"Jocularity, good! We'll require a full measure of it on this journey. 'Til the morrow then, gentlemen. Goodnight," closes McDougal.

At 0600, six bells break the silence of the morning. For good military measure, McDougal has a bugler sound reveille. The first page of the first chapter of a new book is turned.

The "Beast" is slow to respond, but respond she does and gradually picks up speed leaving a haze of black smoke and cinder as the shores of America disappear from sight. The Stonewall, that is, the Kotetsu, is finally, truly underway.

McDougal has carefully plotted his course as practical planning would dictate, but also based on his experiences with the old Home Fleet as a young ensign.

The old Spanish colony of Puerta de Espanas, Port of Spain, now more than sixty years under British rule, is for the most part build on landfill from the surrounding once verdant hills. Indigenous and Spanish bloods call the place of debarkation of the British troops in 1802, Invaders Bay, although it is difficult to imagine the indigenous differentiating between one colonial invader and another. The Spanish colonial governor, at the time of the British conquest, surrendered the city without a fight in exchange for generous terms, a favorite and economical British tactic.

Resupplied and ready, the Kotetsu cruises south away from the hot, humid environs of the Equator. The deepwater bay of Montevideo and its namesake city of San Felipe y Santiago de Montevideo, Uruguay situated on the northeastern bank of the Rio de la Plata, is the next intermediate destination of the Kotetsu. It is planned that resupply here will carry the ship and crew past Argentinian waters, around the Horn and to the small port city of Concepcion in Chile.

Captain McDougal's unusual chain of command and skeleton crew have found a routine and seem to be working together in surprising harmony during these first legs of the voyage. Missing to her "Navy men," however, are the "drum to quarters" drills and live fire exercises of a Man-Of-War. Kotetsu's forward three-hundred-pound Armstrong, muzzle-loading cannon, and two sixty-pound Armstrong guns nesting in their armored turrets, lie silent and ignored.

From Uruguay, Kotetsu cruises along the Argentine coast passing west of the Falkland Islands or Malvinas as these are called by the Argentines. As a young ensign, McDougal's then commander had raced toward the Falklands in pursuit of fur-seal and whaling pirates. To the gross disappointment of all, it was another "competing" U.S. Navy frigate to meet with and engage the pirates, taking them in a near bloodless struggle. Young ensign McDougal and his furious commander had to wait until another day for skirmish and bloodletting, a disappointment to him to this very day.

Blessed with moderate seas and fair skies, the Kotetsu passes through the Straits of Magellan and all the wonders of Patagonia. Smooth black glaciers of lava, long-dormant volcanic ulcers and a denuded, frozen landscape is a beautiful as it is hard. Full ahead, the Kotetsu steams against powerful rolling Pacific waves rising up and clashing with current from the Atlantic. The low-riding Kotetsu, secured and sealed to all extent possible, strains against the pounding onslaught of the seas. To the relief of all, the ship passes the Three Apostles, a rocky and prominent formation off the starboard side, and they are free of the Strait and into the Pacific.

Concepcion, Chile, has few amenities to offer, but resupply and respite from the always challenging seas around the Horn are enough. The officers are eager to push on, so time spend in Concepcion is short. At an officer's call not long after departing port Concepcion, McDougal reiterates the plan.

"Cold currents from the south run with us north along the west coast of the South American continent. We will resupply once more in Ecuador before beginning our tack northwest to Lahina in the Sandwich Islands. I expect fair seas and winds in this part of the Pacific and the crew will, no doubt, be in fine spirits in anticipation of a 'warm' welcome from the Hawaiians. We will not dally in Lahina, however, an extra day or two in port to 'recondition' the ship before our final push on to Japan is not out of the question." Uncharacteristically McDougal smiles before dismissing his officers.

With full coal bunkers and a galley laden with tropical fruits, fish and fowl, the Kotetsu departs Ecuadoran waters as the Galapagos Islands disappear off the fantail. Four thousand miles to the northwest, twenty-two, perhaps twenty-three days cruising, lie the Sandwich Islands, Lahina harbor, island of Maui, royal capitol of Hawaii.

Engineering Officer Edwards looks forward to port of call Lahina. He worries about the French-built boilers manufactured four or five years before and having received no maintenance since. The boilers sweat and weep and leak, causing him great concern as to their continued reliability. He needs forty-eight hours to let them burn cold for inspection and repair. Only fifteen days more to Hawaii!

The big island of Hawaii's Kilauea volcano, with its snow-covered peak, is clearly visible though still a day away. For some, it is difficult to imagine a tropical paradise of mangos and coconuts lying at the foot of its frosty peak. The churning cauldron in its crater constantly oozes forth lava from volcanic wormholes all along its southern slope, which flow unabated until falling, hissing into the sea.

The island of Maui, formerly the haunt of Pacific whalers, and still the capitol of the kingdom, is being transformed into an economy of sugar. Already cane fields, tracks and mills litter its once pristine landscape.

Kotetsu drops anchor off Lahina within sight of the islands of Lanai and Molokai. The old harbor fort fires a single shot in salute to the strange warship flying the American colors. Port duties are assigned and those not so tasked are at liberty to frequent the grog shops and other "seafarer" establishments on Front Street. Gone are the days when half-naked women would swim out to greet happy sailors, but still companionship can easily be found, if only with sporting girls, or an "occasional," that is wives of Japanese, Chinese and Korean laborers working the cane fields. McDougal is pleased but out of superstition refuses to say as much.

Far to the northwest, in the port of Hakodate on the north island of Hokkaido in the Japans, other warships weigh anchor and steam into the Tsugaru Straits east, then southeast into the Pacific. The vessels are the Fujiyama, a wooden-hulled, steam-powered, side-wheeler corvette and the Kaiten, a smaller, steam-driven frigate of the old Tokugawan regime. With Admiral Enomoto Takiaki, a diehard supporter of the Shogunate commanding, the two ships steam into the Pacific on a mission to close with, capture or if necessary sink the Kotetsu.

Chapter Eighteen
A House of God

*E*tsuko is dead, murdered by one of those dispatched to protect Chizuru and her Sisters. The dear and precious presence of Etsuko is lost to them yet they remain bonded together as Sisters in the God of Love.

As the wheels of the oxcarts turn again, they are carried south and away from the cold, harsh waters of Shimonoseki, so do then the wheels of their lives turn new, beginning a life of Sisters forged together by an Omnipresence little understood by any of them.

The irrational enmity of those around Chizuru and her Sisters befuddle them. How can these men hate so passionately these women or the notion of the love of their Creator? Is it the realization that they are not in control that drives this anger?

The Sisters have no dogma. They have no Scriptures. They have only a wisp placed in their hearts by the Creator, a wisp placed in the hearts of all of its creation.

The feral nature of the men around them, the carnal lust in their eyes only serves to bind the Sisters closer and by Chizuru's revelation, further into the bosom of the God of Love.

Slowly, steadily the caravan of oxcarts and escort move south toward Shikimi. In most circumstances the prodigal return of a once married daughter, common or noble, would be viewed with surprise and suspicion if not outright hostility. In the case of Chizuru, however, any hostility is buried under the cover of an imperial decree, though surprise and suspicion remain, without doubt.

Chizuru's father, like many old-regime *bakufu* functionaries, remains. He has been instructed to prepare a suitable residence for his daughter and her, now five, handmaidens. He is not provided with an explanation, and he is not in a position to ask questions. This southern island of Kyushu, as well as the far off northern island of Hokkaido, remains a hotbed of dissent and rebellion. The recognition of and local adherence to Chizuru's imperial decree is as much a test of imperial authority in the region as it is her license to a new life.

After a seemingly unending and anxiety-filled journey, the little caravan halts in front of a small compound. The handsome, if slightly neglected, residence is surrounded on four sides by a low wall and spacious gardens, typical of a higher-level samurai.

There before the gate stands Takeji, Chizuru's father with one other man. She has not seen him since shortly after the wedding or her mother since she left home several years and an eternity ago. It is a formal and slightly awkward homecoming. Takeji speaks.

"Lady Mori, Shikimi is blessed with your return."

Chizuru quickly interjects. "Thank you, Father. But I am no longer to be addressed as Lady Mori. You may address me as Elder Sister Agnes Chizuru." Pointing toward the oxcarts she continues. "These are my fellow Sisters in God."

"I am not sure that I understand, Chizuru, er, I mean Elder Sister Agnes," retorts Takeji.

"In time you will understand. Thank you for the preparations made on our behalf. I will come to you soon."

"As you wish, Elder Sister. A man-at-arms will remain outside your gate at all times for your protection. You may, of course, come and go as you choose. Inform him of any needs you may have."

"We are protected by the hand of God. We shall be better off without your man, but if you are so instructed, he may stay. Our needs are few. Goodnight, Father."

"Goodnight, Elder Sister."

The following days and weeks are busy yet uneventful. The Sisters clean, groom and make ready the old compound, making ready for exactly what they do not yet know.

One Sister, Naoko, is chosen to interface with the village. She exits the compound daily to purchase rice, vegetables and the few sundries required for a measured life.

Inside the compound, much of the grounds become a garden of vegetable and herbs. A few fowl wander freely. On the twentieth day since their arrival, there is a commotion at the gate of the compound. Chizuru is summoned. It is her father. Excitedly he addresses her.

"Elder Sister, this man refused me entrance!"

"Yes, Father. None from the outside may enter our community."

"But he is my man. I am an official."

"No, Father. He is here to protect us. He has been so ordered under my instruction and by imperial decree."

Stunned by the assumed authority of his daughter, Takeji stands for a moment slack-jawed starring at her. After a pause, he regains his composure and remembers the purpose of his visit.

"Yes, Elder Sister. You are correct. I am here to bring you a message."

Chizuru, now gracious, accepts another ornate, sealed envelope, the second in as many months. With a formal "thank you," she retires back into the compound. Chizuru anxiously opens the envelope and reads.

> At the direction and pleasure of his Imperial Highness, a Father Paul Gerard, priest of the Paris Foreign Missions Society of the Roman Catholic Church has been assigned responsibility for your House.
>
> Expect Father Paul to call on you within the next lunar cycle.
>
> As it has been decreed, so is it written.

Far to the north, on the main island of Honshu, former Lieutenant Goemon, captured while in bed, half-naked, is bound hand and foot and taken to the town of Akita, a damp and dreary place on Japan's west coast. There he is arraigned before the local magistrate.

"What is your name?"

"I am Lieutenant Goemon of cavalry, late of my Lord Mori and Hagi castle."

"Your liege lord is dead. You are *ryonin*. You have no master. You have no rank."

"I am *bushi*. I am samurai!"

"You are dog shit! YOU, dog shit, are accused of defying an imperial decree to 'stand down.' You are accused of killing imperial troops. Further, you are accused of illegally entering the residence of a government official, kidnapping and rape. By evidence presented to me, you are found guilty of all counts and hereby sentenced to death."

Goemon seeming not to have heard the magistrate simply says, "I am cold."

"You are cold? Take the brigand away and warm him up!"

Goemon is led outside, down a muddy avenue to its end. Some townspeople have gathered around. A large cauldron sits in the center of a circle of dry wood. Goemon, still bound, is thrown into the pot. The water is cold and he begins to shiver, first slightly then violently.

The kindling is lighted, and fire soon illuminates the square, curls of smoke ascend to the heavens. After a short time Goemon ceases to shiver, he smiles. The warm waters have restored him to sensible insensibility. He realizes again that he is bound and held against his will. He fantasizes of working free of his bindings, leaping out of the pot and scurrying down the road to freedom. He begins to sweat. Soon, Goemon's sweat begets panic. He struggles increasingly against the ropes. His struggles lessen, he begins to moan, then his moans become weeping and an occasional convulsion. His skin parts his flesh, his soul parts his body. Goemon, lieutenant of cavalry, late of the House of Mori, brigand, kidnapper and rapist is dead. How he will be received by his ancestors, only the gods know.

Chapter Nineteen
Feathering the Nest

It is a pleasant and quiet morning. A light breeze carries the calls of birds in the air as Robert Van Valkenburgh takes his daily stroll on a pebbled trail between tall cedars on the grounds of a local *jinja*, Japanese Shinto shrine. Shintoism, an animist religion, though considered pagan by westerners, Robert finds peaceful solitude among the centuries-old trees and worn, near-identical stone effigies of holy men. Upon passing the front of the shrine, its altar vaguely visible within the shadows at the top of stone steps, he bows ever so slightly as if in acknowledgement of the special peace of the place.

"Robert, my friend, is that you?" calls a man stepping out from behind the trees.

Robert is taken back seeing again the handsome face of John Barbour. "What are YOU doing here?" spits Van Valkenburgh.

"Same as you, my friend. I am enjoying a morning stroll on these beautiful grounds. This shrine is many centuries old, you know. It was rebuilt not so long ago by money donated by the Tokugawa. They can be very generous, you know."

"No, I don't know. I have no idea what you mean, what you are talking about. What do you want from me?"

"Have you kept your part of our bargain? Have you written Secretary Steward about the legitimate claims of the Tokugawa?"

Robert's eyes shift. He furtively looks for a way out, either physically or by wit. "Why yes, of course. I did write to the Secretary the very day we made our acquaintance."

"What did you write the Secretary, Robert?"

"Why, I mentioned that factions here are in dispute, and that we should be prudent in not favoring one side or the other."

"Did you now? Is that why you sent your family home? Is that why your residence is now guarded by Marines? Are you being truthful with me, Robert?"

Robert feels cornered by John Barbour's uncanny knowledge of events. He decides to play his hand closely but offers Barbour some scraps of truth. "It is true that I sent my family home. And it is true there stands a Marine guard at the embassy gate. These are tumultuous times, you said so yourself!"

"I see. And what of the Stonewall? You have yet to mention the very point of our discussions."

"I believe that your man or your men have failed. Captain Sugiyama and his interpreter reported aboard the ship and it is on its way here now. They is nothing more I can do for you."

"Interesting. You have already done much for me, Robert."

"I have?"

"Yes, Robert. You have demonstrated that you lack confidence in the Oligarchy. And you have corroborated my information that Captain Sugiyama and his man have reported aboard the Stonewall and that she is on her way here to Japan now. You have been most helpful to us."

"I didn't say all that!" protests Van Valkenburgh.

"How else would I know, Robert? Now calm yourself. You have done well, but there is more you can do."

"More?

"You can, rather you WILL, delay the transfer of the Stonewall to the Oligarchy, that is if she ever reaches Tokyo Bay."

"IF she reaches Tokyo?"

"Never mind that, Robert. That is our affair. You must just simply interrupt the transfer. You can do it. Use some diplomatic or bureaucratic red tape to gum-up the works, delayed instructions and the like. We will take care of the rest. Do you understand, my friend?"

"Yes."

"Good. Now there, placed in the hollow of that stone lantern is the equivalent of ten thousand U.S. dollars in gold *koban*. It is a little down payment and show of our faith in your abilities to get things done."

"Money? Why I cannot accept money from you! From anyone, but especially you!"

"Oh, I think you can. Besides, if someone else were to find it, it would go to waste or maybe a clever man might put two and two together and assume that YOU were paying me for something. Now, that wouldn't look so good, would it, Robert?"

"You, you twist things!"

"No, Robert, there is the real world, then there is your world. You had best wake up to the real world. Take the money. I'm sure you can use. I'm sure your family can use it."

As Van Valkenburgh formulates another objection, his antagonist steps back into the wood and is gone. Alone, he looks around for John Barbour or anyone as witness. For a moment he hesitates and stares at the stone lantern, then he approaches it. With his left hand, he reaches into the rough-cut orifice and extracts a heavy, oil-paper wrapped parcel. He peels back just enough to reveal the bane of man, gold.

As if to ease his conscience, Van Valkenburgh rushes back to his embassy residence, stashes the packet in a bottom, lock-drawer of his desk and pens a letter to Secretary Steward.

Hon. Secretary William Steward

Greetings to you, Secretary Steward. Thank you for your prompt action in regards to my request for embassy protection. The Marine guard took its post some several weeks ago. We are still working out some logistical matters, but I feel the persons and property of the embassy are more secure. It has come to my attention that the previous regime, the Tokugawa Shogunate, wishes the United States to delay the transfer of the Stonewall to the current Meiji government, here in Tokyo. For the lack of some assurances on our part, I fear they may take matters into their own hands, possibly endangering American lives. The old regime still has forces in both the north and the south of the country. To what extent these forces are capable to threatening the current government and/or American property, I am not certain. Accordingly, at least until further information is available, a temporary moratorium on the sale of war material to the Meiji government may be a prudent course of action and keeping with our strict pol-

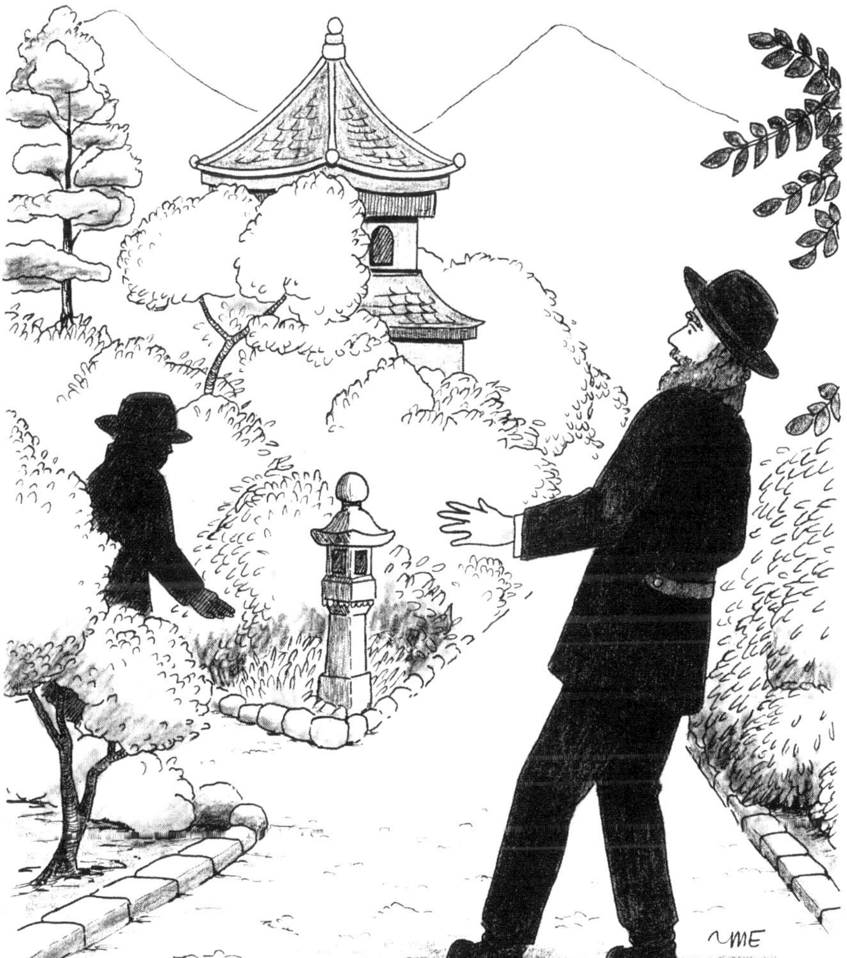

icy of neutrality. I anxiously await your instructions. Always your servant.

*Your servant,
Robert Van Valkenburgh, Ambassador*

Having written the face-saving, possibly live-saving letter to the Secretary, Van Valkenburgh pens a somewhat cryptic letter to his wife.

Dearest Molly,

I pray that you and the children are adjusted back home and in good health. I shall be sending you four parcels, one after the other upon your confirmation of receipt. Do not open these, rather entrust them to Mr. Daniels at Delaware State Bank in Wilmington. I keep no secret from you, let us just say that we are "feathering our nest" against the chance of a new administration and leaner times.

*My love always and to our speedy reunion.
Robert*

Chapter Twenty
An Imperial Navy

The Oligarchy of the "Four" seek to promulgate change, but change requires information and gold. Seventy years later the Chinese revolutionary, Mao Zedong, will write in his Little Red Book that "political power flows from the barrel of a gun." The Four understand this truism, but soldiers need guns and guns cost money. Soldiers too cost money and require orders. Order-givers require information. All this information and gold gathering is a cumbersome process. Only after the mining, taxing and gathering can the debate, decisions, dissemination and action begin.

"Admiral Enomoto assembles a fleet in the north. He commands the corvette Fujiyama, the frigate Kaiten, gunboat Chiyodagata and others. His admirers, followers and numerical strength grow by the day. According to our sources, he seeks to acquire the Kotetsu as well," briefs Okubo.

"Kotetsu! Isn't the Kotetsu on its way here with Captain Sugiyama and Interpreter Ueno aboard?" questions Kido.

"Hai, yes, we believe so," answers Okubo. "The ship departed the American Port of Mobile Bay almost three months ago. We expect she is in or near the Sandwich Islands. We are anticipating her arrival here in approximately three weeks. However, that having been said, we know; 1) a known Tokugawan enforcer followed Captain Sugiyama and Ueno aboard the SS Grand Republic. We managed to get word of this to Sugiyama before its departure, but we don't know what may or may not have occurred aboard or after, 2) another Tokugawan hiree has been spotted with the American Ambassador Van Valkenburgh. Some, but not all of Van Valkenburgh's incoming and outgoing letters have been intercepted and read. It would seem that he is hedging his bets on a Tokugawan return to power."

"Absurd!" screams Saigo. "Admiral Enomoto and his band of diehards returning a Tokugawan to power? If anything he'll hunker down in his far off, frozen Ezo Republic and crown himself king."

"Possible, Saigo, but the Admiral is a clever man, a traditional, if misguided man. Let us not laugh at him."

Kido chimes in. "So long as Enomoto has his 'little fleet,' even tucked away in far off Hakodate harbor, it is a problem and he is a threat. Why, he defies the Emperor he purports to honor. His very presence encourages other malcontents, even those not directly under his banner."

"Gentlemen, gentlemen, please! All of these things are true. We cannot tolerate an Ezo Republic, or a 'little fleet' or an Admiral Enomoto, no matter what admirable attributes he may have. We are agreed on this point.

"We must acquire the Kotetsu and other modern western weapons. We must capture or destroy this 'little fleet' and Admiral Enomoto and his adherents must be brought to heel.

"We shall have one Japan beholden to his Imperial Highness, the Son of Heaven, and one Army and one Navy. We shall have an Imperial Japanese Navy to sweep the seas, first of Admiral Enomoto and others like him, then of the western colonial powers feeding off the bounty of Asia, an Asia rightfully led by Japan."

"And Van Valkenburgh? What of Van Valkenburgh?" asks Kido concerned.

"We do not know more. He was in the habit of sending and receiving his correspondence to Yokohama to be carried aboard America bound ships departing that port. He used one of our men, an embassy worker, as a courier. In this manner, we were able to temporarily waylay his mail, and read some of his letters. Since meeting with this Tokugawan hiree however, a Marine guard has been established at his embassy and the guard now carries embassy post to and from Yokohama. Any protest from us would reveal the obvious," explains Okubo.

"The guard then. Let us protest the presence of a foreign military guard," suggests Saigo.

"Not so easy. First the embassy is considered the sovereign property of the foreign nation. Second, most embassies had already established military guards. The Americans are among the last to do so. Again, interference in their internal matters would result in heavy protests," cautions Okubo.

"We do nothing then?" questions Saigo.

"We have other sources of information and others issues more pressing than Van Valkenburgh's post. Admiral Enomoto seems to have dispatched a significant part of the fleet toward the Pacific."

"What?" cry out Kido, Saigo and Ito. "What is he up to? An attack upon Tokyo?"

"No, we don't think so. He embarked few troops. This is not an invasion. We expect he is going to try to intercept and take the Kotetsu. There is little we can do but hope and wait. The outcome is in the hands of the American Captain, Captain Sugiyama and the gods."

The ad hoc crew of the Kotetsu takes full advantage of the wonders unique to the Sandwich Islands as well as pleasures long known to man wherever he may be. In the pre-contact days of Hawaii, each hereditary chief would dispense justice to those brought before him by the *ilamuku*, a sort of hereditary sheriff. The violator of *kapu akua*, serious crime, or *kapu ali'i*, misdemeanor, would be punished accordingly. By the time the Kotetsu makes port of call Lahina in 1869, the *ilamuku* system had been replaced some thirty years before by a more modern system of police officers and men. In spite of good intentions, and patience on the part of their Hawaiian hosts, the crew of the Kotetsu endeavor to violate as many *kapu ali'i* as possible during their short stay.

"These American sailors display little discipline when ashore," notes Sugiyama.

"I am familiar with their ways. They are easily provoked, fight with little regard to the consequences, and will not surrender the challenge, especially when primed with intoxicating liquors," lectures Ueno.

"Ha, you make them sound like samurai. They have no dignity, Ueno!"

"Do not so quickly pass judgement, Sugiyama. Study your opponent. Know his ways. Is this not the mantra of Master Sun Tzu?"

"Sometimes I think you have become too much like these *gaijin*, Ueno," chides Sugiyama.

"Know your opponent, know his ways," repeats Ueno.

"But we do not contest with the Americans. They seem to be the least objectionable among the *gaijin*. They desire only frivolity and trade. They have, for example, no territorial concessions in China nor in Asia," notes Sugiyama.

"Oh, but they will. They will eventually seek and/or acquire concessions in Asia and we will contest them. I feel this in my bones."

Captain Sugiyama and Interpreter Ueno are standing on the fantail of the ship carrying on a light conversation and admiring the scenery of Lahina harbor when the Captain's orderly locates them.

"Please, gentlemen, the Captain has called for a general meeting of any officers aboard the ship," states the orderly as he turns and departs already seeking others.

Sugiyama and Ueno soon enter the temporary wardroom where Captain McDougal waits.

"Please, gentlemen, sit. We are weighing anchor for Japan in the morning. Please remain aboard the vessel tonight," requests yet orders McDougal.

"Certainly, sir, but I believed that we were to remain her in port for several days," questions Ueno.

"Yes, that was the general plan; however, we have been requested, rather ordered mind you, to leave port as soon as possible. It seems that our crew as well as some of my officers have violated too many local *kapu*, laws. I have been told that my crew is more ill-disciplined than a gang of whalers! By God, it's not true! And we have been ordered out of port by the royal harbor master! In my thirty-odd years in this man's Navy, I've never been ordered out of a port before. What the hell is a *kapu* anyway?" rants McDougal.

Bayard chuckles to himself. "Oh, I wouldn't take it so personal, Captain. Some men just can't handle a little freedom, liquor and tits all at the same time."

"Well, there'll be little fuck'n freedom and certainly no liquor or tits for quite some time to come. I'd guess that the Jappers would just pull out a blade and slice off their *petit*, pretty little, cocks if they caused so much commotion in Japan, eh Ueno?"

"Cock? What is cock, sir?" Ueno asks somewhat innocently.

"Ha, what is a cock? Your privates, man. Don't expect me to show you!" croaks McDougal.

"Ah, *chin chin*, penis. *Wakatta*, I understand. No, no, Captain. Samurai do not cut off penis, samurai prefer to cut off head," comments Ueno.

"Well, in any God-damned case, too many *kapus* have been trampled on, and we're going to comply with the order before our hosts get any more riled up. I bid you a pleasant evening, gentlemen, and please remain aboard."

At six bells the next morning, McDougal wastes no time and weighs anchor, the Kotetsu now finally on his last leg to Japan. All but two sailors have reported back aboard. Those two left behind are incarcerated for fighting and disrespect of a Hawaiian man of some means. It seems that the three hundred-fifty pound local man is the relative of someone important in the royal hierarchy. The man objected to the sailors' solicitous behavior around his wife and cracked their heads like coconuts leaving them prostrate on the street before filing his complaint. Accordingly, the sailors were charged with violating a *kapu ali'i*, disrespectful behavior toward another man's wife. Pleading guilty, the two will be sentenced to serve some months of their life jailed in Lahina before being turned back over to the American Representative Minister. Once repatriated, they can expect little sympathy from either the Representative Minister or the Navy, more probably a summary court martial for "missing movement" and "unruly behavior" and more time in the brig. Woe unto the violator of a *kapu*.

At sea, the rhythms and routine restore the ship's crew to a state or normalcy. McDougal however wishes to demonstrate to crew, officers and official guests that he is in command of a military vessel, not a cruise ship.

"Quartermaster, find me a gunner in the crew."

"But sir, we have no powder or shot aboard."

"I'm not talking about the Armstrong guns. Bayard and I discovered a store of .58-cal. and .30-cal. rounds in the hold while in Havana. We're going to have a good ole-fashioned action drill. Have a box of rounds brought up on deck and find me a gunner to demonstrate the proper procedure and use of the Gatling."

"Aye, aye, sir."

Some hours later, the ship is drummed to quarters. The crew responds automatically but confusion is evident just as McDougal expected and wishes to demonstrate.

"What is your name, son?" asks McDougal.

"Gunner's mate Ryan Borscheid, sir."

"Alright, Gunner's mate Borscheid, let us demonstrate the proper loading and operating procedures of a .58-cal. Gatling gun," orders McDougal.

Officers and crew not having a required battle station are ordered to observe the lesson. Bayard, Sugiyama and Ueno stand by out of curiosity. Gunner's mate Borscheid explains and demonstrates with the assistance of two others he has chosen.

"What shall I target, sir?" asks the Gunner's mate.

"Target? Yes, of course. Acquire one of those camp-followers there. Fire on the hammerhead trailing the ship."

"Yes, sir!" responds Borscheid enthusiastically. "Prepare to fire. Fire!"

Borsheid cranks the handle and seven barrels fire, rotate and fire again in turn. *Pop, pop, pop, pop, pop,* reports the gun. Quickly acquiring the target and range, Borscheid fires again. *Pop, pop, pop, pop.* The targeted shark is shredded by a dozen .58-cal. rounds. The crew cheers.

"All real sailors hate sharks," whispers Bayard to Ueno.

Captain Sugiyama is aghast at the power of the relatively small weapon.

"Ueno, these are our guns. Imagine what these could do to an unarmored sampan or even a wooden ship!" exclaims Sugiyama.

"The *gaijin* do possess scientific and mechanical technologies which Japan does not. Our enlightened Emperor understands this fact," stresses Ueno.

Chapter Twenty-one
The Clash

Fifteen days steaming from Lahina toward Japan, the Kotetsu finds itself thirteen hundred miles northwest of Middlebrook Island, a recently discovered and newly claimed territory of the United States. Eighty years later, Middlebrook Island will be, true to Ueno's prediction, the unlikely site of one of the most decisive naval battles of the twentieth century, the Battle of Midway.

Captain McDougal is satisfied with the crew's response to daily maintenance and emergency drills. The ship itself, with freshly holystoned decks and polished brass, hasn't looked so good since the day she left her French dry-dock birthplace for Danemark in 1864. Damage control and battle station drills have helped to bring together the un-homogenized crew. Only Engineering Lieutenant Edwards seems not to be pleased. Every sea mile seems to fill him with more trepidation. The shortened port of call Lahina provided insufficient time to cool the boilers, conduct inspections and carry out the repairs he had hoped to accomplish. More temporary and half-measures are taken to provide the Kotetsu with standard steaming power.

On this fifteenth day out of Lahina a great puff of black smoke escapes the funnel preceded by a rattle and a bang. Kotetsu's forward speed immediately begins to diminish. The ship has just lost its number-one boiler, maximum sustained speed is now reduced to just five knots.

Captain McDougal shouts into the Gosmer tube, "Mister Edwards, what the hell was that?"

"We just lost number-one boiler, sir. She blew a safety valve. Repairs will commence as soon as able. Number-two boiler is still good. I can provide you with about five knots standard power."

"Very good, Edwards. Keep me informed."

McDougal continues. "Captain Page, would you go below and supervise Mister Edwards? I hope the lad isn't in over his head."

"Aye, Captain, gladly done."

To Sugiyama and Ueno observing from the bridge, he explains, "Captain Sugiyama, it seems we have developed a minor mechanical issue. Our forward progress is impeded, hopefully only temporarily."

"We understand, Captain, thank you," replies Sugiyama slowly.

"How much wind do you figure we have, Quartermaster?" asks McDougal.

"Quartering wind off the port, sir. 'Bout ten knots, sir."

"Very well. Mister Bayard, First Officer Page is assisting below. See that we make sail."

"Aye, sir," answers Bayard with exaggerated enthusiasm.

The order is given, the crew scurries to execute the command. As the sheets are being unfurled aloft, one seaman notices a black smudge on the horizon. He studies the smudge just long enough to be noticed by the Bosun below.

"You there, attention to your task!" barks the Bosun.

"Smoke, Chief. Smoke three points starboard. No sheets or funnel are visible yet."

"Seaman, you are relieved of your duty there. Man the crow's nest. Send that man up a glass! Captain, smoke three points off the starboard bow."

"Very well, Chief. Keep me advised." McDougal turns to the others gathered around him. "Must be the Pacific Mail out of Yokohama? Even with one boiler out, we're closing with her at near twenty knots. She should pass us off the starboard side in about two hours."

After some thirty minutes, the watch aloft in the crow's next reports. "Two ships, four points starboard, Chief."

"Captain, two vessels, four points starboard," repeats the Chief.

"McDougal ponders this new information for a moment, then asks Sugiyama, "Captain Sugiyama, you wouldn't expect an escort, would you?"

Ueno and Sugiyama discuss the question between themselves.

Ueno replies, "No, Captain, and certainly not this far out. Japan's is not a blue water Navy, yet."

"My thoughts also. Is there anything else I should know?" asks McDougal pointedly.

"We were followed onto the SS Grand Republic. Captain Sugiyama repulsed an assault on his person. There are perhaps those who would wish us to fail," states Ueno as a matter-of-fact.

"Wish us to fail? What do you mean? Who?" demands McDougal again, bile rising in his throat.

"There are still some forces loyal to the Shogun which may prefer that the new government not receive this ship, sir."

"These 'forces,' do they have naval vessels?"

"Some, perhaps. Admiral Enomoto is the leader."

McDougal ceases the questioning. He calls to the Quartermaster. "Quartermaster, beat to quarters. This is not a drill."

"Not a drill, sir?"

"No, God damn it, not a drill!"

"Yes, sir. Right away, sir."

McDougal yells into his Gosmer tube. "Edwards, Page, how are we doing?"

"No good, sir. The fittings are corroded and difficult. If we fracture a threaded pipe, then still longer. It may take some time yet."

"We may not have time, Edwards. Damn the threaded pipe. Put your backs into it."

"Aye, sir. We'll give it another go."

"Bayard, I want you to double as Gunnery Officer."

"Gunnery Officer?"

"Yes, Gunnery Officer. Why do I have to repeat myself twice? Supervise the Gunner's mate and his crew. Choose a secondary crew quick for the forward .30 cal. Gatling. We have no heavy ordnance available but if they come close will rake 'em clean."

"Aye, Captain. I'll take care of it," responds Bayard smartly, already trotting toward the Gunner's mate manning the aft .58.

"Captain Sugiyama and Mr. Ueno, please stand by as I may require your assistance."

Within a short time, two warships of the Japanese, pro-Shogunate Ezo Republic close near the Kotetsu. The warship Fujiyama and Kaiten appear battle ready. Fujiyama stands off while the Kaiten approaches with hailing range. McDougal tells Ueno to deliver a preemptory message in Japanese.

"This is the U.S. navy ship Stonewall. Do not approach any closer or you will be fired upon!" yells Ueno into a speaking-trumpet.

Minutes pass. There seems to be some confused discussion among the Japanese on the quarterdeck of the Kaiten. Finally, after some minutes, a reply.

"*Gunkan*, warship, Stonewall. *Kosan shiroo*, Surrender!"

"What did he say, Ueno?"

"He say, warship Stonewall surrender."

"Surrender? Surrender to whom, why?" says McDougal out loud. Quickly he recovers his senses. "Well, I'll be God damned and go to hell if he thinks I'm going to surrender this ship to anyone, let alone that yellow-assed monkey. Don't translate that, Ueno. Just repeat my first warning."

Again Ueno complies with the Captain's instructions.

"This is the U.S. Navy ship Stonewall. Do not approach any closer or you will be fired upon."

As the exchange continues, ex-Captain Page returns to the quarterdeck. McDougal quickly explains the current situation.

"This Japper demands that we surrender. If he approaches any closer or makes any movement with his guns, we'll open fire with the Galtings. Please continue to assist Mister Edwards below. Keep up maximum steam pressure in number-two boiler and stand by for action," instructs McDougal.

Ex-Captain Page disappears below.

Again. "*Gunkan* Stonewall, *Kosan shiroo!*"

Kaiten swivels its forward main gun toward Kotetsu.

"Bayard, open fire!"

Bayard so orders the Gunner's mate on the aft .58-cal. Gatling.

Pop, pop, pop, pop, reports the aft .58, aiming for Kaiten's forward main gun and crew. *Ping, ping, ping, ping*, sounds off the forward .30-cal., aiming for the quarterdeck and Kaiten's officers.

Bayard encourages his crew, "Continue firing at will."

The Kaiten does not return fire. Its forward gun crew is decimated. Several of its officers including the ship's captain are dead. Wounded men litter the deck. Not expecting a hostile response, Kaiten is unprepared and does little in reply. Several of Kaiten's crew return fire with small arms only.

"Quartermaster, 90 degrees starboard, punch a hole in her amid-ships. This is Stonewall's designed purpose you know!"

"Aye, sir. Ram her, it is."

McDougal yells into the Gosmer tube again. "Give me all you got, Edwards. Ramming speed!"

Minutes later the Kotetsu plows toward the Kaiten at the full speed on one boiler.

"Brace for impact!" yells McDougal.

The Gatlings cease fire as the ship's bell rings an alarm. *Klang, klang, klang!*

Kotetsu's iron ram crashes into the side of the wooden Kaiten at eight knots, moving the target ship awkwardly sideways. Her wood breaks and splinters. Men scream. McDougal barks another order. "Full back!"

Kotetsu slowly withdraws its iron phallus from the mortally wounded Kaiten. Kaiten takes on water and begins to list. In spite of the close proximity of Kaiten and Kotetsu, Fujiyama opens fire. A confused volley passes over and around Kotetsu. Kaiten, shielding Kotetsu takes missiles from her own sister ship. Unable to outrun the Fujiyama, Kotetsu loiters just behind the foundering Kaiten. Fujiyama spits another volley, then retires to the northwest. The clash is over. Admiral Enomoto has failed to stop the delivery of the Kotetsu. The new Meiji government will get its ship and the Ezo Republic will fade into history's footnotes.

Kaiten (Ezo Republic)

Stonewall/Kotetsu (USA/Japan)

Chapter Twenty-two
Father Paul

In the small French village of Rochegide there stands a chapel built of stone in the tenth century. Not far above of the chapel is the imposing Chateau de Rochegide, erected some years thereafter and a favorite meeting place for representatives of the monarchy in Paris and the French popes of Avignon in the fourteenth century. It is from this small village surrounded by fields of lavender and cultured vines that Pierre de Garcon later, Father Paul, hails. In that tiny chapel with slits for windows, heavy with incense, and lighted by only a few candles, Pierre would stand with his mother long hours in awe of the mysticism of God before him. So enraptured was he that he voiced no objections when his mother dedicated him to her God and made arrangements for him to join an Order of Oblate Brothers. As a young novice, the Order sent him off to Saarbrucken for education and training. It was there that he truly became one of them and was consecrated a priest.

After much discernment, a regimen of study and training, and years of careful preparation, Father Paul volunteered to journey to the newly opened country of Japan in order to minister to French and other Catholics of the international community and to pursue a personal challenge of producing a credible dictionary of the Japanese language. At that time, he had never imagined being given the honor of supervising the construction of the first "Christian" church on Japanese soil in two hundred-fifty years nor the opportunity to minister directly to the people of Japan.

Far from being intimidated by the daunting challenge, he approaches the task in a pragmatic, step by step manner, while at the same time neither losing sight of his personal goal of writing a dictionary, nor his apostolic mission of witnessing to the Gospel, all while delving into the culture of a previously isolated civilization.

Father Paul's commission from the Oligarchy is not without risk. Spies for competing

factions abound, and outright dissension to the Meiji government is particularly strong in both Hokkaido, base of Admiral Enomoto, and Kyushu near and around Shikimi. Were Father Paul to be too flaunting in his credentials, chances are good that his end would be no different than that of Etsuko.

A message is sent to Chizuru's father, Takeji, both the old regime's and still the Meiji government's functionary in Shikimi. Unexpectedly a courier arrives from Nagasaki bearing a document for Takeji. The message reads.

> A protected guest will arrive in port Nagasaki on the sampan Boekifu. Provide both guard and guide. The guest is to be escorted to the residence of the Sisters of Charity of the God of the Cross. Ask no questions, reveal no presence. You may receive additional instructions at a later date.

Takeji is stymied. No revealing envelope, no honorific salutation or closing, simply a generic *hanko*, signature stamp, used by the Oligarchy. Non-compliance, of course, is not an option. Takeji's head has only remained on top of his shoulders this long because he is known to be pliable.

On the appointed night, Father Paul steps off the gang plank of the sampan Boekifu and onto a wharf in Nagasaki. He wears dark, non-descript clothing of a Japanese merchant. A broad-brimmed hat covers his head and shadows his facial features. Before starting out, he changes clothes again however. Few merchants would walk anywhere near Shikimi, and so that walking the miles to the fishing village will not betray him, he attires himself in leggings, *tabi*, two-toed socks and *warizori*, woven straw sandals typical of the local peasantry.

The small group, guest and escort, set out on the one-two hour walk back to Shikimi. They do not talk and do not gesture, they simply walk briskly in silence. The path is broad and the route is unmarred by obstacles or slope. Quick progress is made. Halting before the residence of the Sisters, the guard opens the gate and moves clear. A door opens, candlelight can be seen but no person. Father Paul enters, the door closes. Takeji returns home clueless.

"God is love. You must love others as I have loved you," gently teaches Father Paul. "Elder Sister Agnes Chizuru, for lack of other followers of the faith here in this region, you and your Sisters must go forth; comfort the poor, minister to the sick, bring hope and the Good News of God's love to the oppressed and imprisoned. Do not cloister yourselves away from society behind these gates. Go forth, be witness to your revelation and to God's love."

Chizuru takes Father Paul's words to heart. It is true, that after Etsuko's death, she had indeed shut the physical gates of the residence, but not necessarily to protect herself rather for the sake of her five Sisters. Now she ponders as to whether she has also shut the spiritual and emotional gates to her heart. Chizuru senses a calling, an inner-voice beckoning her beyond the cloister and into the world full of wrongs and oppressions to make right. She must at least try to change the repressive culture and the unjust world she was borne into. Father Paul's direction is clear. He makes some small adjustments to the inner sanctum of the residence which serves as a chapel, but his manner is gentle, slow and deliberate. He emphasizes Christ as the Servant of the Least. Father Paul writes extensively, asking question after question, not directing as Chizuru had expected.

After a fortnight, he bids his Sisters *adieu*, promising regular visits and disappears into the night following guide and guard and with Takeji trailing behind, again clueless.

Chizuru and her Sisters are inspired. They immediately modify their daily routines from one of discernment and prayer to one of considering first the needs present in those around them. Each morning, except one, in any given week, the Sisters exit the residence. Each carries carefully folded *furoshiki*, Japanese style wrapping cloth, containing *onigiri*, rice balls stuffed with fish and some basic local medicines, teas and supplies. They seek out hungry children, offering food, pleasing worried mothers. They clean and bind wounds, they offer analgesic balms and healing teas. They assist new-born mothers. Never before have these peasants witnessed such selflessness and unconditional love from strangers, strangers from a noble house. Word of this charity spreads. As hopelessness and restlessness begins to dissipate among some, the Oligarchy is pleased, but not all are pleased.

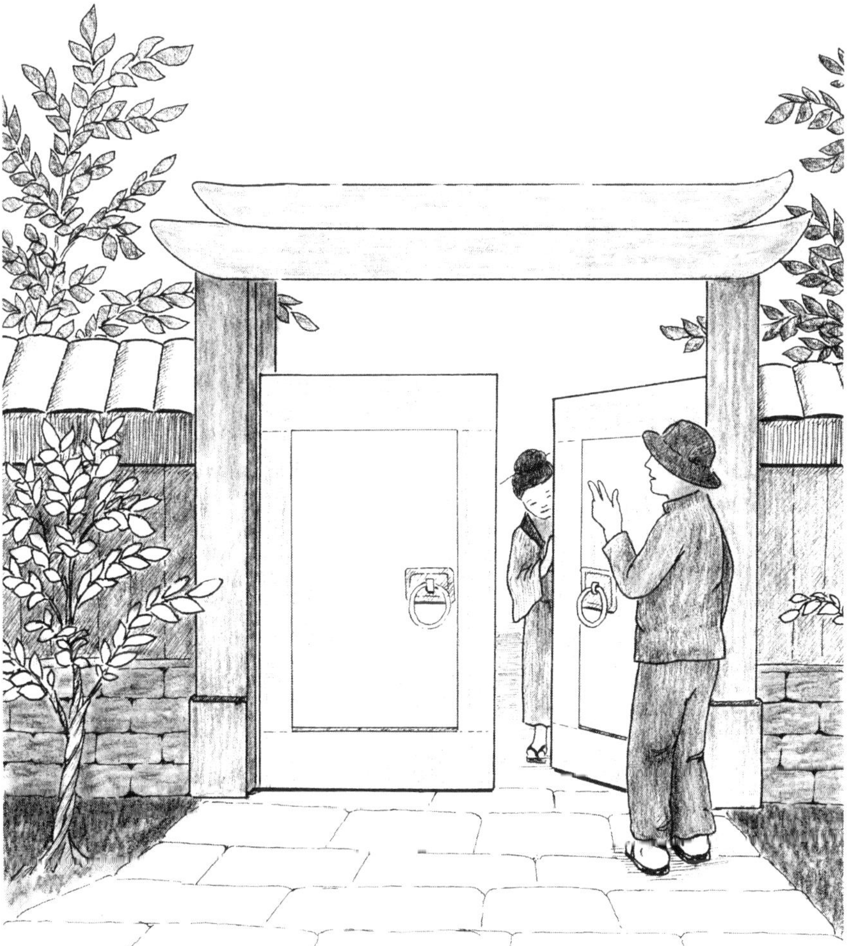

Chapter Twenty-three
Caught in the Middle Again

Van Valkenburgh, never a bold man, finds himself literally boxed-in. He has ceased his morning walks around the grounds of the *jinja* out of fear of another impromptu meeting with John Barbour, so too is he reluctant to dine unaccompanied outside of the embassy. He has no independent news of the Stonewall, so all he can do is wait.

It has been several weeks since Van Valkenburgh's last meeting with the Tokugawan apologist, when a visitor is shown into his office at the embassy.

"A Mister Barbour here to see you, sir," announces Van Valkenburgh's secretary as he shows the young American in.

Ever a bold one, Barbour simply talked his way past the Marine guard, who had no instructions or reason to deny entry to an American citizen, then he requests an appointment of Van Valkenburgh's secretary under the half-true pretense of an urgent commerce matter.

"YOU, how did you get in here?" croaks Van Valkenburgh.

"Why, I was shown in, Robert. I am technically an American citizen, you know."

"What do you want now? I have no information to give you."

"I suppose it is I then who wishes to give you information, Robert."

"So, you have failed then? You failed to stop the Meiji representatives from reaching the Stonewall and now you have failed to stop the Stonewall, haven't you?"

Not registering even the slightest change in expression, John Barbour continues. "The Stonewall will arrive here tomorrow. You must delay her transfer to the Meiji."

"I MUST do no such thing! YOU must leave, sir, or I'll have you arrested."

"Arrested? Arrested for what? I am an unarmed American citizen making a business call on my country's Ambassador. Were I arrested, I would no doubt be questioned. While under the duress of such questioning, I may very well reveal that the American Ambassador has accepted a large amount of money from a foreign government for purposes unclear, or maybe simply reveal that you have been in contact with factions other than those you purport to represent. Which true story shall I tell, Robert? One or the other, or both?" taunts John Barbour.

"You are more incorrigible than Satan himself. What, then, what is it you want?"

"Stop the transfer, Robert. You are a clever man. Find a clever way. If you do not stop the transfer, then I am afraid we bet on the wrong horse. My employers shall be disappointed in me, but much more so in you. I fear the Meiji will somehow discover our little secret. I fear for you, Robert."

John Barbour turns to leave. Van Valkenburgh gasps.

"Where are you going?"

"I am leaving now, Robert. My work here is finished. I am departing on the SS China today. I have other business elsewhere. It is between you and your principals now, Robert. Good day."

Van Valkenburgh is left in his office residence "caught in the middle again." Having already forwarded a portion of his ill-gotten gain to an unsuspecting wife and banker friend in Delaware, the option of simply returning the money to the orifice in the stone lantern is past. The presence or non-presence of John Barbour is no longer an issue. In order to avoid a possible painful revelation, embarrassing recall and inevitable criminal charges, he must think and think fast.

To the north, Admiral Enomoto is facing a similar crisis of his own making. Efforts to stop the Meiji delegation have failed. The intercept and capture of the Stonewall by the task force of Fujiyama and Kaiten has also failed. The Kaiten is sunk and the Fujiyama has returned to base. A complement of sailors and officers are either missing or dead. The Ezo Republic can no longer afford paid intermediaries, bribes and misadventures. The Ezo Republic must resign itself to a more defensive posture and await the inevitable counter-strike by the Meiji, possibly led or certainly supported by the very ship the Admiral has tried so hard to waylay.

Giving up is normally not an option in Admiral Enomoto's playbook, but money is in short supply. John Barbour has disappeared and the opposition grows stronger, more confident by the day. His "little fleet" is not an offensive fleet. The Admiral needed the Stonewall for that. The quick loss of the frigate Kaiten confirms the power and strategic need for such weapons and ships. He sorely regrets sending Captain Kondo on such an important mission. Kondo was impulsive and an idiot. He should have led the task force himself. Better Enomoto lie at the bottom of the Pacific, there is honor in battle. There is even honor in death, a good death.

Admiral Enomoto will wait for the battle to come. He will engage his "little fleet" of sanpans, gunboats and the wooden sided corvette Fujiyama. Admiral Enomoto will be defeated, not by politics but in battle. It will be a good death.

Still he ponders. John Barbour is not worth the effort to pursue. But the American Ambassador and the Stonewall, they both remain valuable targets. Were the American Ambassador exposed for the corrupt petty official that he is, perhaps this would drive a wedge between the Meiji and their American suppliers of material and advisors. No doubt this would at least delay the transfer of the Stonewall. And the Stonewall, safe in port Tokyo, but is it safe? No, perhaps not. Neither the Ambassador nor the Stonewall are safe. If one cannot turn or possess them, then they must be eliminated from the game. This, this would give him more time to deal with the Meiji. The man and the ship, together, within sight of the Oligarchy, he will have to act quickly, time is not on his side. This is not an unanticipated, possible turn of events. A message is set to Ma.

Ascend Mount Hokone

Chapter Twenty-four
Means to an End

"And so it would seem that the gods favor the Son of Heaven," coos Kido.

"It seems to me that the gods favor an iron ship with modern weapons. Enomoto's Captain Kondo is, that is, was an imbecile in trying to strong-arm a seasoned warrior with superior firepower. This is a case in point of our discussions here and negotiations with the foreigners. We must acquire their technologies AND the training to use it. It will take years to fundamentally educate, thereby changing the way our elite class, our leaders of tomorrow, think. *Bushido*, the warrior's spirit, alone is not enough to assume Japanese victories in the modern world," postulates Saigo.

"Well said," adds Ito.

"It is true that emerging from two hundred-fifty years of *sakoku*, isolation policy, will present challenges. It is simply not enough to buy some machines and learn how to use them. Japan itself must evolve and become a modern nation, a nation of enlightened thinkers. Our agenda today however is not of changing a nation, it is of building one.

"With the arrival of the Kotetsu, Captain Sugiyama will be tasked with planning and training for an attack on Admiral Enomoto in Hakodate. Saigo will be in command of the overall operation. Saigo, please."

"Yes, thank you, Brother Okubo. It will be a two-pronged attack. First, land forces under my direct command will be landed north of the city, severing the Oshimahanto, the peninsula on which the city of Hakodate occupies the southern end, from the rest of Hokkaido and where we can expect little or no opposition on the beach. Second, our fleet will stand off Hakodate harbor bottling up Enomoto's 'little fleet.' Should his fleet attempt to leave the harbor, it will be sunk. Additionally, there are defenses in the hills around the city and harbor, these are formidable. As not to incur excessive losses of men and equipment, the city and its defenses must be taken from the rear."

"Very good, Saigo. Once Captain Sugiyama arrives, you and he can work out the disposition of forces, training and the timing," adds Okubo. "We will employ Ueno Jiro in this matter of Ambassador Van Valkenburgh. I trust he will ferret out the facts in short order. Kido, what news of Father Paul?"

"Father Paul busies himself in the building of his church, Brother."

"And his trip to Shikimi?"

"Uneventful. He report that the Sisters are engaged in such activities as one would expect. Admiration among the common people is evident. A sense of stability spreads. Father Paul terms it 'the peace of hope.' There are no Christian converts yet, that we are aware of. Father Paul would take such pride in this eventuality, he would, without doubt, tell me at first chance."

"Ito, anything to add?"

"No, nothing, Brother."

Kido speaks up. "His Imperial Highness is pleased. He anxiously awaits our proposal for the formation of a self-perpetuating, representative government. A government of ministries, debate and laws. Shall we continue our discussions along these lines, Brothers?"

Chapter Twenty-five
The Arrival

The Fujiyama, steaming at battle speed, disappears over the horizon, leaving a scene of waste and death. The Kaiten has also disappeared, slipping under the cold chop of the north-central Pacific in a great hiss and explosion as her boiler gives way. A dome of air breaks the surface, one last gasp of the Kaiten. Danger to the Kotetsu is past.

Flotsam is spread out wide, some before the eyes of the observing crew of the Kotetsu, some already drifting away. Survivors not solidly attached to floating debris, already begin to lose will and consciousness.

Captain McDougal shouts through a speaking-trumpet, "Secure from quarters! Prepare to take on survivors. Lower the whaleboats. Captain Sugiyama, Mr. Ueno, I'll need your assistance as we gather and take on survivors. As enemy combatants, I must secure these men below deck. You must assure them of our good intentions and fair treatment. They are YOUR prisoners, not mine. They will be released to your custody upon arrival in Japan. Do you understand, gentlemen?"

Sugiyama and Ueno respond in unison, "Yes, Captain."

"Very good then. Assist Mr. Bayard. He is responsible for bringing survivors and remains aboard."

Captain McDougal retires to his cabin and begins the sensitive job of writing the ship's log.

> *On February 1, 1869, at approximately 1315, position 19.2796 degrees north latitude, 166.6499 degrees each longitude, USS Stonewall engaged one of two vessels bearing an unknown flag demanding our surrender. One vessel sunk, one retired undamaged. Rescued fifty-one surviving seamen including officers, thirty-three dead recovered. The enemy combatants appear to be Japanese of the renegade Ezo Republic. Prisoners confined below deck, to be remanded to the custody of the Meiji government upon arriving in Tokyo. Japanese (Meiji) government representatives questioning the prisoners presently.*
>
> *Two American seaman wounded by small arms fire, injuries not considered life-threatening. No damage to the Stonewall. No large caliber ammunition aboard, attacked belligerent vessel using .58 cal. and .30 cal. Gatling guns and ram.*

Early the following morning, Captain T.J. Page reports. "Compliments from the Engineering Officer, sir. Reporting number-one boiler repaired and in service. Normal cruise power now available."

"Don't you dare mock me by reporting like a shavetail, Page. This was your ship before it was mine. I could very well be reporting to you if things had gone different at Gettysburg, or Sharpsburg, or Vicksburg. In any case, Good Morning and thank you for making Mister Edwards report."

"And thank you, Captain, for your compassion in regards to our loss."

"It's not a matter of compassion for the South, Page. The South's loss was inevitable, even if it had won the war. It's a case of cultural evolution. A free and industrialized nation is the stronger of the two political species. The evolution yet continues even as we speak. Soon the society and system I know will be gone and something new will replace it. We must continue to live our lives as best we can, without remorse, regret, and certainly not harboring rancor."

"I didn't know you to be a philosopher, Captain McDougal."

"I am a sailor, Page. I am a lonely, old seaman who is long past holding grudges or changing the world."

"A sentiment I share…David."

"The world, this job, my own follies have ground me down. Not polished like a gem, mind you, just ground me down to the dust I will soon become."

I prefer to look at the hour glass of life this way; I yet have time to feel the warm glow of a bourbon, enjoy a pipe of sweet North Carolina tobacco, or share some moments with a willing lady or a friend like you."

"A sentiment I want to share, Page. Perhaps I need to be ground down a bit more," chuckles McDougal.

"So, we just hold this boat together for another few days, off-load the prisoners, and turn 'The Beast' over to the Jappers. Then, I imagine the Embassy is holding some orders for us all?"

"That's my guess," confirms McDougal.

Within the week, the Kotetsu arrives in Japan. Orders are to deliver the vessel to Tokyo Bay, seat of the Meiji government, not to the military and commercial port of Yokosuka, or Yokohama, the former of which having been visited by McDougal some half-dozen years before, then as Commander of the USS Wyoming. McDougal had only been a Lieutenant under Commodore Perry when he last visited Tokyo Bay in 1856, then the Tokugawan capitol of a closed country. Much has changed since then.

On a clear day entering Tokyo Bay can be an awesome sight. To the north lies the Chiba Peninsula, to the south, Tamagawa, the floating world of *ukiyo*, then Kawasaki, Yokohama and Yokosuka. To the west-southwest rises imposing Mount Fuji, the snow-capped, near symmetrically perfect volcano, unofficial symbol of Japan.

As the Kotetsu enters Tokyo harbor proper, McDougal slows the ship to steerage, waiting for the harbor pilot.

"Well, well, Mr. Ueno, back to your old job of 1863, interpreter for the harbor pilot, eh?" jokes McDougal.

McDougal's little joke falls flat. Ueno sees no humor in it. He dryly replies, "No, Captain, that was Yokosuka, this is Tokyo. Then and now have no correlation."

McDougal grimaces, and turns back toward the bridge. He will not attempt humor again today.

Several large wharfs jut out toward the bay in the Tsukiji port district of Tokyo. Along the shore stands warehouses set out in a militaristic, orderly fashion. On the city side of these warehouses, a maze of buildings, structures and streets—organized chaos.

Captain Sugiyama disembarks the Kotetsu in the same formal manner as he embarked. Ueno temporarily remains aboard, as do the Japanese prisoners. The Japanese dead were buried at sea over the objections of Captain Sugiyama. Ueno Jiro remained silent on the matter.

"Captain Page, set a strong watch. No Jappers aboard the vessel without my expressed permission, except, of course, Captain Sugiyama. Crew members not on watch, may stand down. The smoking lamp is lit."

"Aye, aye, Captain," chirps Captain Page.

Speaking into the Gosmer tube, Captain McDougal passes instructions to Mister Edwards. "Well done, Mister Edwards, you got us here. Thank you. Keep one boiler lit for the pumps, let the other go cold. You may conduct maintenance now. I wish to hand over a serviceable ship. Stand by should there be further instructions." He turns to Ueno waiting beside him on the bridge. "Now we wait, Mr. Ueno."

Unexpectedly Captain Sugiyama is not the first to return. Ambassador Van Valkenburgh arrives with a Marine guard. He is ushered into the Captain's presence.

"Good day, Captain McDougal. My name is Robert Van Valkenburgh. Ambassador to Japan."

"Good day, Mr. Ambassador. How may I be of service to you, sir?"

"Yes, Captain McDougal, I am here to remind you that this ship, the Stonewall, is not to be handed over to the Japanese until which time I instruct you."

"Yes, Mr. Ambassador, I understand that this is to be the protocol. When do you expect that to be? I have a restless crew having been aboard ship, more or less, for some months now."

"I do not know, Captain. I await instructions also. I suggest you remain at anchor in the bay."

"At anchor in the bay, Mr. Ambassador. I have prisoners to off-load, coal to take on and supplies to receive if the ship is to remain under my command."

"Argue with me and the ship will not remain under your command, sir."

"Mr. Ambassador, I have my orders too and you sir are not in my direct chain of command. I will off-load my prisoners, send them to your embassy if you so desire. I will take on coal, as well as water and victuals. Then, when I am good and ready, I may heed your 'suggestion' and anchor in the harbor awaiting further written orders from proper naval authority. Do not press me, sir!"

Van Valkenburgh taken back by McDougal's resistance to political intimidation replies, "Very good then, you understand my directive."

"Dually noted, Mr. Ambassador," replies McDougal coldly.

Van Valkenburgh scurries away, anxious to extract himself from another sticky wicket. Not long after, Captain Sugiyama returns with an armed escort. The escort waits impatiently on the wharf as Captain Sugiyama boards the Kotetsu.

"Captain McDougal, sir. I am prepared to take charge of the Ezo prisoners."

"Very well, Captain. They are yours. Mr. Bayard, have the Bosun assist Captain Sugiyama with the prisoners."

The prisoners are bound, single file on a long rope. They are led from below deck, onto the main deck, then off onto the wharf where they squat surrounded by unsympathetic looking men. The pitiable prisoners are eyed suspiciously by their guards. Soon they are led away and out of sight, en masse, to a temporary stockade in one of the dark, damp warehouses along the waterfront.

"Captain Page, set a double watch, as well as both Gatlings manned and ready. Don't be obvious about it, just make certain that the guns are loaded and a crew is nearby. I just don't have a secure feeling about things. The Ambassador was nervous and everyone seems to be on edge. I take it Japan is not yet as stable as they would like us to believe."

The first night, then day passes peacefully. The crew carries on mostly routine duties discreetly stepping around the watch and Gatling crews. On the second night, just after three bells, the aft watch alert the Officer of the Deck.

"Lieutenant, sir, I heard voices out in the bay."

"Native fishermen perhaps?"

"Perhaps, sir. But these voices were hushed."

"Voices from the bayside, you say."

"Yes, sir. That is what is strange. I don't see anything."

"I agree, strange. I'll inform the Captain. Bosun, pass the word, gun crews man your guns."

Suddenly and before the Captain can be awakened, a point in the bay, aft of the Kotetsu, from where the voices emanated, there is a *swoosh*, followed by a bright light. The light becomes larger and brighter, it is a great fire. The watch, accustomed to the dark, collectively blink their eyes to adjust.

Captain McDougal and Captain Page arrive on deck.

"What is it, Lieutenant? Report!" barks McDougal.

But before the Lieutenant can utter a word, one of the watch screams, "Fireboat! Two fireboats aft, drifting toward us."

"A page right out of the Spanish Armada," snorts McDougal. "Well, I'll be no Duke of Medina. Page, get Edwards to run up steam on number one and fire number two. Prepare to get underway. Cast off!"

Mr. Page calls to the Quartermaster, "Beat to quarters!"

Almost simultaneously, lines are cast off, the left screw begins to turn in reverse and the crew runs to each's battle station. Fortunate for the Kotetsu, the aft Gatling is the .58 cal. gun and can readily engage targets aft.

The Kotetsu slowly moves in reverse, not having full steam pressure even in number one. The Gunner's mate orders the aft .58-cal. to open fire. "Open fire! Fire at will!"

Pop, pop, pop, pop, reports the .58 at point-blank range. The deadly spray of lead, however, does not slow the fireboat. It continues a lifeless drift toward the Kotetsu, the arsonists long before leaping into the waters of the bay and swimming for shore.

There is a sharp crash and jolt. The first fireboat has hit the Kotetsu on the starboard aft side. Unlike the Spanish Armada, however, the Kotetsu is iron not wood. Also, she has less tar, rope and sheets on deck. The little sampan just bounces off the iron Kotetsu, dropping some small burning debris on her deck. At battle stations already, the fire crew aboard the Kotetsu work quickly to extinguish the flames using her steam-powered water pumps. Sir Francis Drake would turn in his grave at his brilliant tactic of 1488 being so easily foiled by the modern technologies or iron and steam.

Having bounced off the Kotetsu, the first fireboat is deflected and burns harmlessly in the harbor. The second fireboat however, having missed its moving target crashes into the wharf causing a great conflagration. Soon the fire spreads and engulfs several of the warehouses lining the shore. The fire begins to burn out of control.

Kotetsu withdraws to the middle of the harbor, and watches the circus intently. The ship does not anchor and the crew remains battle ready.

On the wharfs and along the harbor, highly organized and skilled fire brigades soon arrive. Bravely, the brigades battle the flames, but with only buckets and pikes, it takes time until the last of the flames can be extinguished.

Dawn breaks on a burned and scarred waterfront. Captains McDougal and Page stand together on the weatherdeck, as Thomas Bayard step up to join them. "Good morning, sirs. Welcome to Japan!"

Chapter Twenty-six
Bittersweet Return

Walking along and through the fire-razed area of the port, Ueno comments, "What have they accomplished, Sugiyama? The Kotetsu remain unscathed at anchor, a wharf unusable, a half dozen storehouses burned. Ugh, for the sake of the gods it smells as 'scorched meat' around here!"

"Yes, the scorched meat of fifty-one sailors and officers sent on an ill-fated mission, plucked freezing from the cold waters of the Pacific, saved only to be consumed in flame a few days later. Not for the sake of the gods, Ueno. How cruel are the gods to allow man his folly! What have they accomplished? They have sealed their own doom. The Oligarchy now has no option to negotiate. The Oligarchy must now destroy the 'little fleet,' kill Admiral Enomoto and eliminate the Ezo Republic from the annals of Japanese history. And worst of all, after two hundred-fifty years of peace in Japan, I fear it will be I who is burdened with the breaking of that peace," laments Sugiyama.

"I fear your assessment may be correct, Sugiyama. I was just thinking about what part I may play in this unhappy affair," says Ueno.

Sugiyama hails two *jinrikusha*, human-powered, two wheeled cab, and they return to the *ryokan*, Japanese style inn, where they will remain until summoned.

The arrival of the Kotetsu has resulted in even more angst for Van Valkenburgh. On the surface of the affair, he should simply welcome the officers and men to Japan, collect the $500,000 in gold *koban* from the Meiji government and release the warship to their keeping. He, however, has bargained to defraud his own government in a convoluted scheme whereby a lesser sum will be paid in exchange for future coaling and supply concessions from which he and his partners will profit for years to come. At the same time, he has been bribed by the old regime for information and to create quasi-legal disruptions and delays in the transfer of the vessel to the Meiji government. The Meiji government, the renegade Ezo Republic and his potential business partners all demand comeuppance, none of which he can deliver.

A summons is received at the office residence of the Ambassador.

"Mr. Ambassador, a message, sir," announces the ambassadorial secretary.

"Open it! Read it! Do your job, man!" demands an agitated Van Valkenburgh.

"Yes, sir.

```
Ambassador Robert Van Valkenburgh, Representative of the United States of America. You are summoned to appear before the ruling council on this day. Be prepared to present documents to close the sale of the
```

> USS Stonewall to the Meiji government of Japan, as per the terms and conditions previously negotiated. Also, you are entreated to discuss additional technical assistance and training as pertains to the USS Stonewall but also future cooperations."

To himself Van Valkenburgh just moans. "Had I only been the true and faithful servant of my country. Now, I have dug my own grave!"

At anchor in Tokyo Bay, the USS Stonewall sits and awaits her disposition. Even without the rhythmic droning of her engines, the pounding sound of waves against her hull and the constant three dimensional motion of being underway, understood only by sailors, general routine aboard ship is little changed. True, after the fireboat attack, vigilance remains high. The watch is yet doubled, her Gatlings are locked and loaded, and fire hoses lie like waiting serpents about the deck yet these are but small inconveniences to a crew largely unemployed except for fishing and playing cards.

McDougal paces the weatherdeck. "Damn this waiting. Damn that spineless political hack! Are there no men of principal in government?"

"If it makes you feel any better, David, the Confederate Navy was worse. No money, few supplies and a representative government of one—Jeff Davis. At least you have an entire Administration and Congress to blame. Besides, isn't it a sailor's right to complain?" calmingly notes Page.

Bayard sees an opportunity to glibly add. "Always the gloom and doom, Captain. Just think, your pay, sea pay at that, just piling up in the Paymaster's office. And maybe, if Ueno can bribe an official or two, we may yet get ashore to visit the wonders of Yoshiwara. You've been to Japan before, Captain. Have you ever had a Japanese girl?"

"Thomas, you don't query a gentleman about the whereabouts of his 'privates,' unseemly discussion!"

"End of this discussion perhaps, Captain, but I can see that Captain David S. McDougal shouldn't take up poker in his retirement. You wear the answer all over your face—sir."

"In truth, I will miss your jocularity, Bayard. You are a good man, a brave man under fire but most of all I'll miss your witticisms and unique way of viewing and confronting issues," confesses McDougal.

"It is a hard thing, Bayard, when a man reaches the zenith of his natural usefulness to society. I no longer propagate the species, nor can I claim the strength and agility of a young man. These past few years I have lived by my experience and wit. But this too is soon coming to a close. I will be retired soon upon my return to the United States, not by choice, but at the pleasure of politicians who recognize that younger men are now better suited than I. Politicians who themselves neither retire nor recognize their own aged irrelevance. It is a bitter-sweet moment in a man's life, Bayard, to become free of the shackles of servitude, yet having no real purpose but to await the inevitable arrival of disease and death. I've seen it so many times before. I shall not bemoan it however, it is our fate. It is the fate of all creation."

In the old Odawara castle, the present seat of the ruling Oligarchy, Saigo seethes, "The blotched murder of our representatives, the attempted piracy of our warship to be and now the burning of our docks and warehouses here in Tokyo. These counter-revolutionary elements must be eliminated immediately."

"Agreed, Saigo. We are all in agreement. It is just a matter of timing. The Admiral has spent himself. For lack of a treasury, he can hardly afford to feed and clothe the troops he has. The few malcontents seeking refuge with him are more of a burden than adding to military strength. His 'little fleet' consists only of one capital ship now that the Kaiten is lost. The few other gunboats and sanpans hardly constitute a major threat to us. We have a blockade and invasion plan, you, yourself have prepared it. We will attack with the advantage in both fleet and marines. Our force will be multiplied by overwhelming superiority in modern weaponry, if the Admiral's Republic doesn't implode in the meantime," lectures Okubo.

"All of what you say is true, Brother. *Bushido* dictates a separation of one's self from emotion. Patience, spirit and skill will ultimately prevail. Forgive my outburst. I shame myself," apologizes Saigo after a rare moment of self-reflection.

"No at all, Saigo. We all understand the urgency of consolidating our revolutionary gains and we share your frustrations with the Admiral and his minions. All in good time, Saigo, all in good time."

Chapter Twenty-seven
Only Touched Once

The enlightenment of the Meiji reverberates across the Japans. In the old feudal system, social strata dictated that, no man was lower than a merchant. In the new Japan, however, these now unemployed and masterless samurai are forced to seek sustenance, they themselves become this social pariah. *Bushido* and Confucian ethics are a barriers to brigandry, but the samurai, as a class are restless, some restive under the new regime.

So it is with the peasantry also. Previously little more than human fodder in war and dirt grubbers in peace, the worth of a great lord used to be counted in how many peasants his holdings could sustain. To summarily execute a man, a head of household with mouths to feed, was of absolutely no consequence. The offending man, woman or even child, may have simply not bowed low enough to suit the lord as he passed by.

To say that the peasantry was suddenly emancipated by decree is incorrect. The common man, however, is no longer considered property of sub-human value in that the great fiefdoms of the country have been dissolved. This human waste was simply ignored by the noble and warrior classes, whether prosperous or starving.

Humankind, by nature, is self-serving. In times of prosperity more hedonistic pursuits become the norm, whereas in leaner years, the stone pathways leading to the shrines of the gods are worn smooth by the sandals of the faithful.

Hope is a powerful concept. Men defy monsters clinging to faith based on hope. In this new age, the Sisters of Charity of the God of the Cross bring a hope to the peasantry of Shikimi and its environs. Each morning, the Sisters rise, briefly freshen, then they gather for meditation and prayer. Neither Father Paul nor Elder Sister Agnes Chizuru taught them this discipline, perhaps it is one of the seeds planted by the Creator and sprouted in the breasts on men? After Morning Prayer, they clean and tidy the residence house, each to her particular chore and strength. The morning meal is *gohan*, steamed rice, with *tsukemono*, pickled vegetables and if they are so blessed, a fish multiplied, a gift from a friendly fisherman or monger.

Before going out, each Sister, by her own inner calling, makes simple food, *onigiri*, rice balls with seaweed, pickles or fish, handcrafted and packed. Medicines are prepared from local plants and herbs. *Akashiso*, red Shiso leaf, is picked and squeezed for its dull red juice which lowers blood pressure in the elderly. Papaya leaf, similarly prepared is used to reduce fevers brought on by foul humors common to stagnant waters. The juice of the creeping vine stops blood flowing from a wound or birthing mother either on contact or in a tea. The pulp of the vine being applied to the wound to promote healing and reduce scarring. Many such remedies, common and uncommon, are employed by the Sisters in their ministrations to the people. All such remedies are available to those who make study of the Creator's masterful abundance and gifts.

There is no more heart-rending sight in this world than a hungry or sick child. There is no greater compassion than comforting the sick or the dying. It is in these manners that the Sisters witness to the love of the Creator, attracting in the process other like-minded young women and impressing the symbol of the Cross into the hearts of all who stare in wonder at the unknown adornment girded around the waist of each of the Sisters.

Written and revised histories are unknown and unavailable to the common people who can neither read nor write, even among the Samurai class. Oral histories, testaments and legends passed down over nine generations however, recall a time when others in Japan followed the God of the Cross, believed in hope and love and were exterminated by crucifixion for their faith. The people thirst for hope, want to believe in a better life, but are tentative and afraid.

"Sisters, we have accomplished many wonderful things in our mission here in Shikimi. But our work does not end. Our work here and elsewhere in Japan will not end with us or those who may follow us. There will always be need; the hungry, the thirsty, the sick and the dying. But our greatest obstacle is fear in the hearts of the many and fierce pride in the hearts of the few. Pray that an inner peace may radiate from our hearts, serving to balm the mortal fear and break-down the pride of the foolish.

Already my body grows old and tired. You are not slaves to me but my friends. If your heart speaks to you, follow it. You are free to go or stay, follow your hearts."

"But Elder Sister, your revelation? Must we not follow the revelation?" questions a Sister.

"By the love of the Creator, I was touched once, but only once in my consciousness. I can provide you no more guidance than that which has already been placed in each of your hearts. Do not blindly follow me or worship me. I am a false god. I struggle as do you. Follow the Spirit which created you and all things. Stay or go, but always remain in the love of the Creator. This is the will or the Creator and my command. Now, let us go in peace in the service and love of the Creator."

Elder Sister Agnes Chizuru retires to her small, barren room and writes.

Oh hear me, for here I am,
lost in the confusion of human endeavor.
Chosen by revelation of the Creator,
only touched once but for a lifetime.
Guide me for I am blind.

Chapter Twenty-eight
The Politics of It All

Ma has returned from Canton. He is aware that the Stonewall is anchored in Tokyo Bay, he therefore reasons that his bar room hirelings have failed to stop Captain Sugiyama and his man. Admiral Enomoto's mission to take the Stonewall as a prize on the high seas, as well as last night's attempt to burn her while lashed to the wharf have also met with no success. The Admiral's failures are not Ma's concern. It is Ma's reputation that concerns Ma. It is by his reputation that he fills his rice bowl each day. His reputation must be preserved.

Ambassador Robert Van Valkenburgh dresses in his best formal attire for the summons before the Ruling Council. As he fusses with clasp and pin, he mumbles to himself, rehearsing a litany of honorifics and excuses. "I can work through this. They cannot possibly know anything about my private correspondence, and there was no one else on the shrine grounds. I am the American Ambassador, I am above suspicion and above reproach," he states, satisfied with himself.

"Billy, hail a *jinrikusha*. It is time for me to go before the Council."

Billy Watkins, the secretary to Ambassador Van Valkenburgh steps outside of the embassy residence and into the street. He raises his hand. Fortunately but unusually, a conveyance waits on the side of the street next to the embassy.

"*Taishi wa gaimusho ni tsurette itte kudasai*, please take the Ambassador to the Foreign Office, demands Billy of the *jinrikusha* man using his very best standard Japanese.

"*Hai, wakarimashita*, yes, understood," replies the man.

Van Valkenburgh exits the embassy walking confidently, trying not to betray the great anxieties welling up inside him. He seats himself comfortably as the man centers himself between the shafts of the conveyance. The man lifts and pulls into a trot, they are off. The conveyance starts down the street at a lively pace, rushing air passing through the cab and cooling Van Valkenburgh's sweaty brow. For the first time in a long time, he pushes aside his worries and enjoys the leisurely ride. Not paying close attention to the route himself, the *jinrikusha* man veers down a narrow alley. The conveyance stops and tilts down as the man sets the shaft down on the ground and steps aside. Van Valkenburgh forms a question as both anger and bile well up in his throat.

"What the bloody hell are you doing, man?"

The *jinrikusha* man pulls a *tanto*, short sword, from inside the folds of his *hapi*, type of short jacket adorned with celebratory or advertising symbols or slogans, and smiles. The futility of resistance and his end has not yet entered Van Valkenburgh's mind as he utters out loud. "Oh for the sake of God, the politics of it all."

Even before the sentence is dry on his lips, the *jinrikusha* man thrusts the *tanto* into the side of Van Valkenburgh's neck, piercing his jugular on the left side. He then pulls the knife across his throat severing vocals, esophagus and windpipe. The stunned, late Ambassador, unable to even gasp, stares at his assassin for a moment, gurgles and then is no more.

"The Ambassador dead?" stutters McDougal.

"Yes, sir, yesterday. He was murdered by a *jinrikusha* man for reasons which are unclear. He was not robbed, nor did the murderer make any effort to flee. He was arrested, of course, and executed this morning."

"Well, the Jappers certainly don't fuck around, do they?" comments McDougal dryly, trying to process the information.

"No, sir, they do not," responds Billy Watkins trying to cope with the disaster. "Ambassador Van Valkenburgh was en route to the Foreign Office to discuss the transfer of your ship among other matters," states Billy. "What shall we do, sir?"

McDougal calls for Mr. Bayard. "Thomas, let's get that Japanese friend of yours, Mr. Ueno and Captain Sugiyama as well. We need to sit down and have an ole-fashioned pow-wow." I think you as a civilian representative of our government, should lead the negotiations in the stead of the late Ambassador Van Valkenburgh. Besides, it was your idea and letter that started this whole process almost two years ago."

"Billy, get Mr. Ueno and Captain Sugiyama over here chop chop. We'll let them unravel the complexities of protocol and the meeting."

The next day, Captains McDougal and Sugiyama sit with Ueno and Bayard in the captain's cabin aboard the Kotetsu to discuss the matters at hand. Ueno Jiro, knowing his expressed inside link to the Ruling Council, agrees.

"It can be done!" announces Ueno confidently.

Sugiyama, unaware of Ueno's inside link, is less confident. "Ueno-san, do not misrepresent our positions here," whispers Sugiyama into Ueno's ear.

"Do not be concerned. There is a way," replies Ueno curtly.

"Very good, then. Until the appointed time and place," McDougal closes, thanking his Japanese guests.

"Thank you, Captain, we will meet again soon, I think," says Ueno as he bows.

For three days McDougal and his staff aboard the Kotetsu wait for a reply from the Ruling Council and Ueno. On the third day, without prior notice, Ueno pulls alongside of the Kotetsu in a small boat and waves them aboard. Irritated by the short notice, McDougal and Bayard scramble to change into appropriate attire, McDougal's dress uniform and subdued brown wool suit respectively, and climb aboard the small boat.

"So sorry, Captain. The Council considered our proposal for two days, then just replied 'come,'" explains Ueno.

"Come?" questions McDougal.

"Yes, just come. This 'come' is translated, 'now, without delay.' If we are to hope for a positive session, then we must go now and 'without delay.' Captain Sugiyama will join us there."

Bayard interjects. "Thank you, Jiro. I know you did your best."

The highly anticipated meeting, on both sides, flows smoothly. Honorifics, even pleasantries are exchanged, highly unusual for the Ruling Council. Also, condolences are expressed by the Council in regards to the death of Ambassador Van Valkenburgh and assurances that the crime has been investigated and the murderer punished accordingly.

"Captain McDougal. On behalf of his Imperial Majesty, allow me to express our sincerest regrets about this unfortunate incident and assure your government of the safety of its diplomats and citizens living here in Japan," states Okubo elegantly.

"Thank you, your honor. I shall convey His Majesty's sentiments and your assurances to the proper authorities."

Okubo continues. "As for the matter for which we are gathered, we propose; the immediate transfer of the vessel to the government of Japan. The previously agreed amount of $500,000 in gold *koban* shall be deposited with your embassy here in Tokyo. Second, your officers and crew are hereby released to return to your country. Lastly, we have officially requested of your embassy and hereby request of you personally and directly, that you, Captain McDougal, as well as a select group of officers and men, remain in Japan for a period not exceeding one year for training and technical instruction in the usage, deployment and tactics of the Kotetsu.

We are prepared to be generous in exchange for your verbal agreement and best efforts. "Captain Sugiyama personally requests you, the Hero of Shimonoseki."

"Thank you, your Honor. I am greatly honored. I was not aware. Ambassador Van Valkenburgh said nothing to me."

"Captain McDougal, how shall I say? We suspect that your Ambassador, Mr. Van Valkenburgh, may not have always been working in the best interests of either your country or ours."

"I am greatly saddened to hear of your suspicions, your Honor. Candidly, however, if this were true, it would answer a great many questions. Please allow me a day or two for consultations with those whom I would choose and with Mr. Watkins at the embassy," replies McDougal.

"Granted. Session adjourned," announces Okubo abruptly, smiling ever so slightly.

Chapter Twenty-nine
The End Game

"How many years have we struggled to bring ourselves, our ideas, our people to this fulcrum in the history of our nation? We, Brothers, all sired and raised, in a rich and ancient culture mired in Tokugawan feudalism, self-isolated from all other humanity. We Four, and others, circumvented the law and courted death in seeking enlightenment abroad. Now, by the grace of His Imperial Majesty, we are tasked to build a modern nation, respecting its inspiring past but driving it forward to a future where the genius of the Japanese people may be liberated from its serfdom to ancient ways, thereby becoming an example and the natural leader of all colored peoples of Asia. This is our destiny!" lectures Okubo.

"Since the restoration of His Imperial Majesty to his rightful place as the spiritual leader of our nation, we have accomplished much. But as in the labyrinth of human development, each new discovery leads on to three more…."

"What is your point today, Brother? Nothing in this homily is new to us," questions Saigo somewhat bored with it all.

"My point, Brother Saigo, is just this. We, Four, are burdened with an impossible task. Each step we take toward liberalization and representative rule begets three more contentious issues."

"Yes, this is already known to us. What are you getting at?" asks Kido, beginning to understand.

"The unifying spiritual commonality of our society resides in the person of His Imperial Majesty. I propose that we beseech the Emperor to make a public proclamation to the nation."

"But His Imperial Highness has never, in the recorded history of our nation, made such a public proclamation. It would expose him as interventionist, fallible—human!" cautions Kido.

"Perhaps, but wasn't the *Sonno Joi* movement about restoring the sovereignty of the Emperor? How can one be sovereign in silence, Kido?"

"Were the proclamation carefully crafted, it may very well create considerable disunity and weaken the resolve amongst the counter-revolutionary elements currently arrayed against us," continues Okubo.

"Not to mention our critics," adds Ito.

Okubo continues. "The Tokugawans seek to control the emperor, not defy him. And as you point out, Ito, our efforts at political structuralization and legal liberalizations would be greatly simplified if the Imperial Throne were seen as the guiding influence."

"A brilliant but dangerous political envelopment," compliments Saigo.

"For the sake of the nation, and for the sake of the Japanese people, I am certain that His Imperial Majesty will give the Council's request utmost consideration," assures Kido.

"All agreed then?" proposes Okubo.

"*Hai*, yes," reply all.

A proclamation from His Imperial Majesty Meiji.

> To the people of the Japanese nation be of strong heart, for in the chronology of our people there have come times of sacrifice and change. Today, we stand at a great door which we have already opened but not fully entered into. We are called to an opportunity to integrate our nation into the family of nations thereby assuring the propagation and strengthening of our race, ideas and customs. To not enter this opened door condemns our people to a future of the past and decline. Class and title divide a people, divisions beget resentment and war. We are of one blood. May the gods grant us to become of one mind and one purpose.
>
> This is the will of your Emperor.

"The proclamation is to be read in every village and town throughout the land each day for one lunar cycle. Let the people discern the will of His Imperial Majesty," proclaims Kido.

"The proclamation and an offer of peace has been sent to Admiral Enomoto in the north and also to his allies in the south. If, by the last reading of the proclamation, the Admiral has not responded, then we will attack," reports Saigo.

"Very good then. Captain Sugiyama and McDougal have prepared the fleet?" queries Okubo.

"Yes, Brother. The fleet is prepared for blockade and bombardment. My invasion force is readied for the assault from the north against Enomoto's rear. I assure you all of a great victory."

"Never underestimate your opponent, particularly an opponent who has few options," cautions Kido. "A cornered enemy is most dangerous."

"I do not underestimate the spirit and cunning of the Admiral. He shall be overwhelmed by a combination of our newly acquired technologies and the 'hammer and anvil' tactic of our forces, a maneuver similar in many ways to that used by Julius Caesar against the Egyptian Army of King Ptolomy nearly two thousand years ago," boasts Saigo.

"The Admiral will not expect such an attack?" questions Okubo.

"The Admiral does not have the benefit of a European education, Brother. He has never read Julius Caesar's Commentaries or studied his tactics. We shall prevail," reiterates Saigo with certainty. "After the fall of Hokodate, I expect resistance in Kyushu will dissipate if not disintegrate."

"And Father Paul, his church and followers?" queries Ito.

"The foreign missions are exceptionally pleased with the church, Brother. And Father Paul is exceptionally pleased with his small flock, including the Sisters in Shikimi."

"What of our man Ueno?" asks Okubo.

"The Tokugawan assassins have rendered his mission against the late American Ambassador null. As you know, Ambassador Van Valkenburgh is dead. Information about his suspected activities, while interesting no doubt, is less important now. Ueno will accompany Captain Sugiyama and the American advisors on the

Hokkaido expedition," continues Saigo. "He is known to the Americans and may be useful should the Admiral seek to negotiate rather than die."

"Very good, Brothers. This is the end-game then. Let us begin to discuss new business such as the proposed *kokukai*, Diet or Parliament, system," announces Okubo.

"Long live Greater Imperial Japan!" cry all.

Chapter Thirty
The End of the Beginning

Ueno Jiro finds himself in familiar surroundings. Captain Sugiyama has positioned himself stoically on the bridge of Kotetsu as she steams out of Tokyo Bay. Standing beside Captain Sugiyama are Captain McDougal as well as the civilian Thomas Bayard, only today it is THEY who are the observers and advisors to the Japanese. Captain Page declined to further assist his non-white, comrades at arms, a slight not quite well understood by the equally xenophobic Japanese. The scene of departure is well imprinted in Jiro's mind, but the passage, blockade, battle and aftermath have become more of a blur than a clear memory of the events.

Vague recollections of a loud blast, a tremendous wave of hot air and then—silence. Days and nights, nights and days, recuperation slower than time. Not quite fully recovered, now he is unable to continually update his skill set and constantly reestablish his credentials with an ever-younger line of bureaucrats and keepers. He still receives a small stipend and is consulted, although less and less frequently, until his irrelevance becomes self-evident.

Relevant or irrelevant, this all depends on a point of view. Many years past, a priest had admonished him in saying, "All gods matters, just as all men matter." This thought, among other thoughts, snippets and memories, the mental litany of his life comfort and satisfy him in his eighty-ninth year. He sits on a comfortable *zabuton*, traditional Japanese cushion, sipping hot *sake*, rice wine, at the hearth of the house of his father. Here the memories of his mother, his brothers, his first travels overseas in the warship of the *gaijin*, foreign, Commodore Perry, as a functionary of the *bakufu*, Tokugawan bureaucracy, and years in the governmental organs of the Meiji Emperor, warm him. These fill him with pride and satisfaction. He closes his eyes, smiles and passes from this world to the next.

Chapter Thirty-one
One Last Hurrah

Captain David S. McDougal files an official request for furlough with Mr. William Watkins, Acting Ambassador of the United States Embassy in Japan. Before relinquishing command of the USS Stonewall, in official capacity, he grants extended leaves to those officers and crew members he has chosen to assist with the 'training' mission to the Japanese. The remaining officers and crew are given passage on the new SS America and return to San Francisco and their naval duties. Thomas Bayard, under no strict orders, chooses to remain at the Captain's side learning more about Japan, while under the tutelage of Ueno Jiro in matters of customs and language.

After several months of preparation and training, the Ezo "problem" in the north can wait no longer. Under orders, Captain Sugiyama, Commander of the Task Force K assembled to blockade the Port of Hakodate, steams out of Tokyo and Yokosuka north to Hokkaido. Task Force I follows Captain Sugiyama's force by a half day, consisting of screening vessels and the invasion force under the direct command of Acting General of the Army and Ruling Council member Saigo.

McDougal is elated to be participating on the mission and in preparing Captain Sugiyama's crew for action. In his many years of naval service, he has, with the exception of the Shinmonoseki Incident, really only been involved in minor skirmishes at sea and longs for a "real" engagement. Bayard is less enthusiastic about fighting, but is thoroughly enjoying his sojourn as an advisor to the Japanese.

The blockade of Hakodate harbor is successfully established, and Task Force K patrols the entrances to the harbor while awaiting General Saigo's invasion force landing and advance toward Hakodate for the action to begin. Once Admiral Enomoto and his force of three thousand Shogunate diehards realize that defeat is at hand, he may try to run the blockade and flee, in lieu of surrender.

General Saigo finds that Admiral Enomoto's fortifications, even on the north approach, are more formidable than expected. It takes more than a week for his forces to slog their way through these, one at a time and begin to threaten the main bastion at Hakodate.

One morning a lookout aboard the flagship Kotetsu spots smoke rising from the "little fleet's" funnels, a good indication that preparations to get underway are being made. A short time later, the Admiral's shore batteries open fire on the Task Force K, Sugiyama's blockading ships.

As McDougal leaves the bridge and goes below to coordinate naval gun fire, the bridge of the Kotetsu is rattled by an exploding shell. Sugiyama is killed outright. Ueno lies wounded. Remarkably, Bayard is only dazed, wandering about the damaged bridge trying to provide assistance where he can.

The ships of Task Force K return effective fire onto the "little fleet" and shore installations. The Admiral's fleet is unable to break the blockade and is defeated in the environs of Hakodate harbor. On June 27, 1869, Admiral Enomoto surrenders to General Saigo. He is arrested, charged with high treason and returned to Tokyo in chains. The Ezo Republic is dissolved.

Returning to Tokyo, McDougal and Bayard complete their work for the Meiji government. While awaiting passage to San Francisco, Bayard proposes a weekend excursion to Yoshiwara.

"What do you think, David? This will be our last chance to see, smell and taste the fruits of old Japan. Things will change even more rapidly now that the Tokugawan diehards are defeated."

"I already know what 'fruits' you want to taste, Thomas. Yet, maybe a little distraction would do me good too. I suppose we should go. Were ole Pryun here, he would have already packed my overnight bag for me."

The short journey to Yoshiwara, south of the Tamagawa River is a pleasant one. Both men make the very most of the weekend, enjoying all that the aging district has to offer.

McDougal's tryst lays the seed of a future generation, in the form of a son whom he will never know of or meet. Yet his half-Japanese son will learn of him, and spend a lifetime in researching and emulating his naval career and adventures.

Soon after returning to the United States, Captain McDougal is promoted to Admiral and retired. Never a slight man, "The Admiral" has outgrown both uniform and Sunday best. A loose-fitting shirt and overalls now suit him best. Swollen ankles and shortness of breath indicate that he is worn-out on the inside as well. Death should come painlessly one night. Suddenly, the comforting thought is punctuated by throbbing and a sharp pain in his head. He loses control or consciousness and finds himself prostrate on the floor of the porch unable to move or even cry out.

David whimpers in pain. Drool mixed with tobacco juice and blood seep from his mouth. He has injured himself in the fall. He soils himself. Death does not appear on cue, night falls. He is cold. Morning does not come, only fleeting memories of soldiers, sailor and marines he has seen, contorted crumpled, prostrate as he, on the battlefield and deck.

Ultimately we are all dead men. He dies just before dawn, not lost at sea or in a tomb of the unknown, but on the fertile ground which is his beloved Maryland.

Chapter Thirty-two
The End of Innocence

The pragmatism of Father Paul was in itself an act of God. Although he visited the Sisters of Shikimi from time to time, his visits were often more for his own spiritual good, than to guide or instruct the Sisters of Charity of the God of the Cross. He recognized that somehow these Sisters led by Sister Agnes Chizuru, though ignorant of the Scriptures and without Church dogma, had grasped the essential concept of the Christian life. They honored and loved their Creator as they loved and served its Creation. For an "untouched" man, even his consecrated servant, he felt it to be morally impossible to question those chosen by revelation and "touched" by the Creator's hand.

Father Paul chose to expose only new novices to the more orthodox practices of St. Joseph's Catholic Church in Tokyo. In this manner he slowly supplanted the quasi-Catholic-Animist views of his flock in Shikimi with the more mainstream dogma of the Roman Catholic Church.

Sister Agnes Chizuru ages gracefully. She outlives Father Paul, most of her original Sisters, the Oligarchy and two Emperors. In 1926 the new Emperor, Hirohito, has just ascended the

Chrysanthemum Throne. As a "Victor" Nation, Japan is basking in the post-World War I feel-good years. Japan's foreign relations are at a relative high point, its economy and people prosper.

Sister Agnes Chizuru of the Sisters of Charity of the God of the Cross celebrates her sixty-first year within the peaceful subculture which is the convent and her eighty-sixth year of life. In her lifetime, she has witnessed and lived through monumental changes in Japan. Since her birth in a small village near Nagasaki, Japan has evolved from a feudal state, survived revolution, seen its Emperor restored to power as titular head of state, established a modern parliamentary system of government, and become a respected member in the family of industrialized nations. But most importantly, Sister Agnes Chizuru has lived to see the Christian faith return to Japan after almost two hundred-fifty years of being forbidden, persecuted and driven from its shores. Her heart leaps with joy as young novices freely enter the convent and professed Sisters busy themselves with their work in the surrounding villages as well as Nagasaki. Many of Sister Agnes' original members, consisting entirely of her handmaidens at Hagi Castle have already passed away. The simple white crosses in the courtyard bear silent witness to their years of work and prayer. Sister Agnes Chizuru herself has relinquished title and responsibilities as Prioress or Elder Sister as she prefers. She eats little, speaks less and spends hours in quiet contemplation and prayer.

On a quiet winter's morning, she kneels before the altar, in the unheated, stone-floored chapel. Sister Agnes Chizuru praises God for the blessing and wonders she has lived to see. She draws from deep within to expose her transgressions. She struggles to clearly identify sinfulness in her words and deeds since her last confession in prayer. Her mind wanders. She is so tired.

Later that day she is discovered, eyes closed, body stiff, kneeling in supplication. Without sin, and by Grace, she has passed from this world to be with her Creator. She has truly gone in peace to love and serve the Lord.

Chapter Thirty-three
Shifting Sands

"Charles E. DeLong is to be the new American Ambassador," announces Kido.

"And what do we know about him?" asks Okubo.

"We know he practices law in his own country, and has served as a Representative in his home region, the new State of California. It is said that he is strong-willed, and speaks rudimentary Chinese."

"Chinese? This Charles DeLong is a white man?" queries Okubo.

"It would seem so, yes. There are a great many Chinese in California. He seems to have learned Chinese for reasons of trade. He operated some type of merchant business in the gold-country of California. Ueno knows nothing of the man," continues Kido.

"Thank you, Brother. Enough of the American, we can judge for ourselves soon enough," states Saigo.

"Brothers, we have come far. Our nation is not the same nation as we were born and raised in. We have accomplished much since the collapse of the Shogunate but as you are all aware, we cannot evolve in ignorance. We must further educate ourselves as to the world around us. We have all agreed on the dissolution of the *han*, clan, system and the establishment of a representative form of government. Yet there are many examples of governing bodies around the world. We have purchased modern arms from the Prussians, fine ships from the Dutch, machines from the French and British, railroad and communications equipment, as well as general trade with the Americans, but our exposure to their home countries, government, tax systems and general commerce is quite limited.

"It has been proposed that WE conduct a great mission, an embassy, of our top political and academics in a world tour of industrialized nations. Iwakura Tomomi has been chosen by His Imperial Highness to lead this embassy. Iwakura has likened the undertaking to the great embassy of Peter I of Russia in his quest to modernize his country in the eighteenth century. WE, Brothers, as vice-ambassadors, have been asked to accompany the Iwakura Embassy, since it is we who will have to develop state, encourage private institutions and form a governing body upon our return," outlines Okubo to an apprehensive Council.

"Brother Saigo, you are to remain in Japan. You are our Acting General of the Army, and one of this Council. You are to be charged with maintaining the peace and stability of the nation in our absence. This is the expressed will of His Imperial Majesty. Is this not so, Kido?"

"Yes, Saigo. His Imperial Highness has great faith in you and admires your ability to cut through the fog of matters and get things done. You are greatly honored," comments Kido.

"I am humbled that His Imperial Majesty should consider me. And I am relieved that it is I who may remain here in my country and with the Army. I only wish the late Admiral Sugiyama were here with me."

"Yes, it was only just and right to promote him after his great victory at Hakodate. He was a fine officer and sorely missed by all. Ueno Jiro will also remain here in Tokyo. His wounds are healed but he is not the same man. Both his eyesight and hearing were affected by the blast, and he is infirm. He however remains a worthy advisor on foreign matters," finishes Okubo.

"Let us then commence our preparations," says Kido.

"Yes, the preparations will take many months, and the embassy itself at least two years. May His Imperial Majesty have patience with us. Long live His Imperial Majesty!" exclaims Okubo.

"*Banzai, banzai, banzai,* hurrah, hurrah, hurrah!" shout all.

Epilogue

This story, *Legacies Are Forever (Book 3)*, like *The Search (Book 1)* and *From Across The Waters (Book 2)*, is a factious tale. Having said such, however, allow me to expound on some interesting facts.

The odyssey of the CSS Stonewall is historical, as are many of the places, people and events used as the framework of the narrative.

In 1868, the United States did sell the ex-Confederate CSS Stonewall to the Meiji government of Japan.

The Stonewall was built in French shipyards and armed by English foundries, but the sale to the Confederate government in Richmond was cancelled as the Confederacy began to crumble.

The Danish government stepped in to purchase the ironclad, but later suspended the contract due to gross inefficiencies of the design as pointed out herein.

Confederate Naval Captain T.J. Page finally did acquire the ship on behalf of his government, but never fired a shot in anger. He abandoned the vessel in Havana harbor in 1865.

The United States government eventually acquired the ex-Confederate vessel from Spanish Colonial authorities for a cash payment.

After the overthrow of the Tokugawa Shogunate, Iwakura, Okubo, Saigo, Kido and Ito each played prominent roles in the new Meiji government. A so-called Oligarchy played a short-lived transitional role in Japan.

In 1868, Christianity was de-criminalized in Japan and the Catholic church of St. Joseph was established in Tokyo.

Admiral Enomoto, founder of the Ezo Republic failed in his counter-revolutionary attempt to reestablish Tokugawan rule.

The Ezo Republic warship Fujiyama was captured by Meiji forces and the Kaiten was sunk, her captain and much of her crew being killed by Gatling gun fire.

Captain David S. McDougal retired as an Admiral of the U.S. Pacific Fleet.

Robert Van Valkenburgh replaced Robert Pryun, and became the first U.S. Ambassador to Japan. He was recalled as Ambassador under circumstances that are not historically clear. I am certain that the Ambassador was an honorable man, but in being appointed by the corrupt Johnson/Grant administrations, I have taken liberties. Also, my personal gross distaste for politicians of all persuasions and their appointees is evident here.

Thomas Bayard was Assistant Secretary of State to Secretary Marcy before, served in the U.S. Navy during, and remained in government service after our Civil War, or as I prefer to called it, a more Southern sympathetic term, "The Struggle."

The Pacific Mail Steamship Company was one of the first regular passenger service lines of the Pacific, primarily between the United States, China and Japan.

The geography and chronology of the story are generally correct and accurate.

I hope that you have enjoyed *Legacies Are Forever* and this trilogy series. God bless you all.

Vocabulary

French –
Adieu – lit. to God, farewell
Du jour – Daily
Legion d'Etangere – French Foreign Legion

Hawaiian –
Ilamuka – Hereditary sheriff of the pre-contact kingdom
Kapu ali'I – Misdemeanor
Kapu akua – Felony

Japanese
Akaoni – Devil-like demi-god
Akashiso – Red Shiso leaf
Bakufu – Tokugawan-era bureaucracy
Banzai – Hurrah
Boekifu - Tradewinds
Bushi – Warrior
Bushido – Warrior code

Daimyo – Lord
Edo jidai – Edo era
Furoshiki – Japanese-style wrapping cloth
Fundoshi – Japanese-style loincloth
Gaijin - Foreigner
Gaimusho – Foreign Office
Gomen nasai – Sorry
Gunkan - Warship
Hai – Yes
Hai wakarimashita – Yes, understood
Han – Clan
Ichibu – Tokugawan-era silver coin
Jika – Hometown
Jishin – Earthquake
Kaigunkyoku – Navy Department
Kamizashi – Japanese-style hairpins
Katana – Japanese long sword
Kannoshi – Shinto priest
Koban – Tokugawan-era gold piece
Kokukai – Diet or Parliament
Kosan shiroo – Surrender! (Imperative)
Kun – Honorific informal
Michinoku – lit. End of the road district in northern Japan
Omedeto de gozaimasu - Congratulations
Omikosan – Priestly attendants
Onigiri – Rice balls stuffed with fish or other
Ri – Unit of linear measure, 4 km
Roju – Tokukawan era ruling council member
Ryojin – Elderly person

Ryonin – Masterless samurai
San – Standard honorific
Sama – Polite honorific
Sayonara – Goodbye
Samurai – Warrior class
Sakoku – Tokugawan era isolation policy
Sake – Rice wine
Seiza – Formal sitting
Sengoku – Japanese Civil War
Seppuku – Ritual suicide
Sonno Joi – Revere the Emperor, expel the barbarian movement
Tabi - Traditional two-toed socks
Taishi wa gaimusho ni tsurette itte kudasai –
Take the Ambassador to the Foreign Office please
Tanto – Short sword
Tofu – Bean curd
Tsunami – Tidal wave
Tsukemono – Pickled vegetables
Ukiyo – Floating world
Warizori – Woven straw sandals
Yushima Seido – Tokugawan era school for bureaucrats
Zubuton – Traditional Japanese cushion

Spanish
Castille – Fortifications
Hasta manyana – Until tomorrow
La Guerra de los diez anos – Ten Years War
Los Contras – Rebels
Los Yanquis – Yankees

Papito - Daddy
Sangria – Fruited red wine
Señor – Standard honorific
Si – Yes
Tapas – Hors d'oeuvres